The Lost

of

Sherlock Holmes

As Recorded by
John Watson, M.D.

By Alex Prior

Copyright © 2020 Alex Prior

ISBN: 9798551458661

PUBLISHNATION
www.publishnation.co.uk

For my mother, who also wrote a book, and for my children Charlie and Jamie, who have also detected the genius of Holmes all by themselves.

Also with thanks to my wife Emma, Claire Robins OBE, my Padlins friends, the Brethren at Manor Court, and anyone else my less than Sherlockian memory may have omitted.

The game is afoot. Again.

Publisher's Foreword

To describe these cases as 'lost' is perhaps a degree of poetic licence. They were not lost in the traditional sense but rather forgotten by most, other than those who have been granted special access to Scotland Yard's archival files.

During my researches into a series of unconnected cases, I was made aware of their existence by one of the archivists whose name I have agreed not to share here. I am indebted to her for her kindness in retrieving them and producing facsimile copies of the original handwritten manuscripts for me.

I was surprised to learn that the cases contained herein have been used and referred to for the development and training of investigative officers over many years, a purpose of which I am in no doubt Sherlock Holmes himself would have approved.

I have selected six cases from the number available to me. While four of the narratives are relatively short, as were the majority of Watson's transcriptions, two detail much more substantial cases and are included in their entirety. With regret, I have not been able to include cases such as "The Adventure of the Master Mason", "The Puzzle of the Little Key", or "The Deplorable Case of the Belgian Ambassador", perhaps they are for another time. However, I commend those presented here as both informative and entertaining to students in the art of detection.

Doubtless, some of the language, prejudices and attitudes contained herein are a product of their time and may seem unenlightened to our more evolved sensibilities, However, they are reproduced here unexpurgated for authenticity.

Finally, I am grateful to Scotland Yard itself for permission to publish them for a wider audience of Holmes' aficionados to enjoy.

Any errors in transcription are solely my own.

Alex Prior, November 2020.

Contents   **Page**

The Adventure of the Old Acquaintance

I note from my journal that the temperature had exceeded ninety-two degrees Fahrenheit according to the mercury thermometer mounted upon the wall of our sitting room. London sweltered and sweated under the stifling onslaught of the sun's unremitting rays.

I had been trying to amuse myself with a novel while Holmes was slumped in his chair, thumbing through a pile of foolscap. Even he, who usually seemed immune to extremes of temperature, was looking a trifle listless. Neither of us had enjoyed our cigars; the humidity and stillness of the air had robbed us both of that small pleasure. The last remnants of the smoke still hung in the air, adding to the sensation that we were slowly choking for lack of oxygen.

'I say, Holmes, do you…?' I was arrested by his hand gesturing for silence before I could suggest a walk to the Serpentine for a little cooler air.

'A letter, unless I am mistaken,' said he, stirring from his repose.

I had heard nothing, but now a slovenly step could be perceived upon our stair accompanied by a faint jangling. Presently there was a knock on the door and, at Holmes entreaty, a flushed Mrs Hudson ushered in a profusely sweating messenger. Holmes signed a receipt and bade the bearer leave.

After scanning the missive quickly, he threw it across to me. I found myself hoping it was a call to action; anything that would require a break in the monotony of our routine would be most welcome. The paper was heavy, of good quality and embossed with a crest I did not recognise.

My dear Sherlock,

Despite our lack of recent contact, I feel that I still know you, so avidly have I followed your exploits in the press and periodicals. However, until now I never once entertained the notion that I should require such services as you render.

I am at my very wits' end and have no one to turn to for solace. The matter is delicate and of great personal importance.

I beg that you might see me and furnish such advice as you see fit. I shall call at three o' clock this afternoon.

Your friend in need,
Frederic Bagshot

Immediately my interest was piqued. I knew so little about Holmes' personal life before we met that I must admit to a certain less than truly honourable concern for the writer of the note. Here was an opportunity to learn a little more about my friend, a pursuit of which I never seemed to tire.

I looked up to see Holmes smiling at me with a twinkle in his pale grey eyes. 'So Watson, you think that here is an old compatriot of mine whom you might press for a little salacious tittle-tattle at my expense?'

A guilty look must have passed across my face, although I am sure Holmes could not have perceived the blush due to the ruddy complexion forced upon my countenance by the heat.

'Why, Watson, you look like the guilty schoolboy caught by a master with his hand in a fellow pupil's tuck box!' Holmes laughed. He seemed genuinely amused at my discomfort. Not for the first time I had reason to wish my companion's powers of perception were a little less acute.

'I'm sorry, Holmes.' I tried to convey the right tone of humble apology. 'I should never wish to pry into your affairs.'

'Nonsense, my dear chap! You should be intrigued by such a note as there are many features of interest about it, aside from the text itself. In point of fact, the writing is less enlightening than the paper upon which it is written.'

I had become so accustomed to our little routines that I knew Holmes was waiting for me to play my part. I considered the note again. 'I see that the paper is expensive and of a fine grain. The pulp from which it is made is perhaps of a specific tree?' I hazarded.

'Excellent, Watson! You have excelled yourself on this occasion. The paper is indeed of a most unusual type. And it is made from the pulp of a very particular tree.' He cut himself short by glancing at his pocket hunter. 'It is almost three, and I think I should save a few of my

3

observations for the benefit of our most esteemed guest. Come!'

His decisive tone rang out upon the last word, and the door opened to admit a dashing, debonair man in his late thirties. Holmes roused himself from his chair and bowed perfunctorily to our visitor. I scrambled to my feet to follow his lead, although I had not yet been introduced.

'My dear Holmes, you have changed little and yet seem taller than I recollect.'

'And you, my dear Lord Freddie, look rather shorter to my eyes.' Both men smiled, and Holmes then amazed me by grasping the man's hand and embracing him. I had never seen my friend moved to such an overt display of affection before; indeed, Holmes would usually look disapprovingly upon such unseemly conduct.

'Watson, allow me to introduce Lord Frederic of Bagshot.' It was now that I recalled the title. Lord Freddie, as he was universally called, was a well-known patron of the arts and often referred to in the gossip columns and society pages as among England's most eligible bachelors.

Lord Freddie nodded to me and held out his hand. Holmes waved him to a chair. 'I see your recent travels have proved a most rewarding experience. How did you enjoy the Philippines?'

His Lordship gave a visible start and then smiled. 'Ah, Sherlock, I see nothing escapes you. You were always quick on the uptake, but I see that the years of practice have honed your skill.'

The small quick smile on my friend's lips did not escape my notice. Holmes, although he would rarely admit it, was quite susceptible to sincere flattery.

'Regretfully I take it your transit on the clipper was less than satisfactory. The accommodation inferior, and the captain of the ship unwelcoming. If only the ill news had not been quite so pressing, you might have made more suitable arrangements but family misfortune always requires the most immediate attention.' Holmes paused for effect and reached for the cigar box.

Lord Freddie was staring hard at my friend. 'Who told you? I have endeavoured to keep the affair from outside ears. Does the press know? How can this be? It must be one of the servants!' he cried in obvious distress.

Holmes held up his hand in a placatory gesture. 'Have no fear. No one has told me of your situation. I deduced by your complexion that you had been abroad and in a hot clime. The paper upon which your note was written is a very particular type that is only produced in the Philippines, made from the manoao tree that is cultivated only there. The paper has been infused with a strong scent of tea. Had it been transported here for sale, it would have been in sealed containers and untouched by the odour, therefore it was transported in personal luggage by you. Your cabin must have been close to the hold where the tea was stored, therefore it was inferior accommodation. The captain appeared unwelcoming because he failed to secure you better, or offer you his quarters as your title befits. You must have been determined to return to these shores as expeditiously as possible or you would have waited for

5

another ship. What could cause you to fly so? Surely only bad news of a nature such as a family tragedy could elicit such a result.'

'Remarkable. Quite outstanding, Holmes, you are correct in every respect! Such a *tour de force* confirms to me that you are the one man in England who can shed light where until now there has been only darkness.'

'Well then, old friend, pray tell us of these singular circumstances that have brought you so many thousands of miles to our humble abode.' Holmes settled back into the plush, his eyes half-closed and the cigar slowly consuming itself in his left hand.

'I must confess it will be a relief to tell it, but I fear the machinery that brought such a tale to this state may be so obscure as to confound all reason. I was, as you said, engaged upon a visit to the Far East. I had been away some six months and travelled with my batman and personal secretary to India and thence to China and the Queen's colony of Hong Kong. After a stay over of some six weeks, we ventured on to Manila. It was there that word reached me of a shocking turn of events at my ancestral home.

'My father, a vigorous and energetic presence, had collapsed one afternoon while taking his usual promenade in the garden. He was carried to his bed and has since become a meek and timid man. He will not speak of the matter and refuses to leave his room. Further, he will not see my sister or myself, nor any of the domestic staff save for Bennett, the family butler of many years standing. I fear my father has lost his mind, Holmes, I really do! He refuses to eat food prepared in the kitchens, even though it is excellent, and insists upon simple fare brought daily from the local hostelry in the nearby village of Chesterford. Of course, the locals are beginning to talk, and ugly rumours have begun to circulate.'

'What is the nature of these rumours?' Holmes asked quietly.

Lord Frederic hesitated, then composed himself and continued in a bitter voice. 'In centuries past there were some instances of insanity in my family. The rumours say my father has succumbed to a curse that was placed upon my ancestors two hundred years ago when the fifth duke killed a local man in a duel who had accused him of an indiscretion with a serving girl.'

'I see. And you say your father has not ventured forth from the house since that fateful afternoon?'

'No. Not to my knowledge.'

'How many staff do you have in your household?'

His Lordship looked surprised and then thought for a few moments. 'I should say forty in the main house. Then there are perhaps twenty in the grounds and many hundreds more on the estate farms.'

'Thank you. Yours is, in essence, a simple problem although there are some features of interest. Still, I feel compelled to ask you: do you want me to expose the truth, regardless of what manner it may take?'

'Holmes, I must know what lies behind this if I or any of my family are to have peace of mind again.'

'Even if the results may not be of a nature you should welcome?'

A brief moment of doubt seemed to pass across Lord Freddie's face before he was once again resolute. 'Even if that be the case.'

'I shall certainly look into the matter. Please return to your father and take care to inform him by a note that Watson and I shall be with you later this evening.'

When Lord Freddie had been shown out, Holmes sat in thought for ten minutes, a fresh cigar wreathing his sharp features in smoke. Experience had told me not to intrude upon his mental activities, though I confess Lord Freddie's story had left me with an abundance of questions. It seemed apparent that my friend, with his incomparable experience and knowledge of human peculiarities, saw clearly where to me there were only swirling mists.

'It is a sad story, Watson, and I fear little good will come of it for the reputation of the family. There is a scandal here, and Lord Freddie may emerge a man lowered in status, but greater in means more personal. Would you be so good as to send for a cab? I think perhaps a high tea at Alanson's before the five thirty-three from Kings Cross.'

*****

8

The village of Chesterford is of a significant size but still considerably smaller than the ancient nearby town of Saffron Walden. As the dogcart my friend and I shared drove from the station toward the ancient pile, we passed through fields ablaze with the yellow crocus flower that has been cultivated in the area since Roman times. I remarked to Holmes upon the fine selection of follies visible from the road. It was obvious that not only had the Bagshot family lived here for many generations but also their ancestors had enjoyed considerable wealth.

It was as we passed along a lane lined with impressive horse-chestnut trees that Holmes broke the silence he had maintained during our journey thus far. 'You know, Watson, I see much similarity between the fruit of these noble trees and the little problem upon which we are presently engaged.'

I considered the comment then asked my companion to elucidate.

'Surely you see, Watson, that like the chestnut, unyielding and painful on the outside, there exists within the beauty of a stout heart!'

I admitted that I failed to see the comparison of which my friend propounded.

'Come, Watson, can it be that you have not yet penetrated to the core of this matter? I see that you have not. Well, I am sure that we shall not be detained here long and all shall become transparent in a matter of hours.'

Our driver took us down a long, straight drive leading to the grand house. As we traversed the ornamental bridge spanning the lake, we gained our first glimpse of Bagshot Hall. It was indeed a most impressive country seat. Undoubtedly it was of ancient origin, but it had been added to continuously over the years with a taste and restraint so often lacking in comparable properties.

A footman waiting at the entrance called inside and within moments Lord Freddie was flying down the steps to meet us. 'Thank goodness you have arrived. My father has taken a turn for the worse and we have called for the family physician. Upon my return here I sent up a note, as you instructed, and received word that my father had screamed when he read it then collapsed sobbing upon his pillow. What should I do, Holmes? What can be done?' His Lordship was clasping and unclasping his hands as he spoke and it was obvious that he was on the brink of despair.

Holmes laid a hand on his shoulder and spoke in the soothing voice of which he was so capable when required.

'You must trust me, my friend. I believe this matter can now be brought to a conclusion without further delay. I will speak with your father alone. Please summon the butler – Bennett, wasn't it?'

Bennett proved to be a small man but with an obvious military bearing. His face betrayed his concern and his eyes looked hopefully at my companion.

'Take my card to the Duke immediately. Inform His Grace that I must see him now, and that it is in his interest that I so do.' The butler needed no further bidding and returned within minutes to confirm that the Duke did indeed desire to see Mr Sherlock Holmes at his earliest convenience.

Holmes turned to Lord Freddie. 'This will not take more than ten minutes. While I am gone, please gather together all domestic and grounds staff that were appointed during your absence and have them assemble in the drawing-room.'

It was nearly a quarter of an hour before Holmes returned. His face gave no clue as to the nature of his interview with the Duke. His mouth was set in a firm line and he strode purposefully into the drawing-room. 'Will all domestics take to the right side of the room and all groundsmen the left?'

There was muttering and bustling as the dozen or so staff followed his orders. Holmes inspected each one carefully before selecting a cook, who could have been no younger than sixty, and a gardener of about the same age as Lord Freddie. The rest of the staff he dismissed. He strode to the windows and looked out upon the lake until they had gone.

Suddenly he turned upon his heel. 'Your name?' he barked at the cook.

'Somersham, sir,' she returned in a somewhat belligerent tone.

'And yours?' He looked at the younger man.

'Westbridge, sir.'

'Do you know each other?' Holmes' tone indicated that he already knew the answer.

'No, sir, not before we took our positions here,' said the cook.

'No, no, this really won't do. You are mother and son, are you not?'

The gardener looked ashen and gazed at his feet. The cook looked furiously at Holmes. 'And what business is it of yours, Mr Busybody?'

'Blackmail is the business of all law-abiding subjects, Mrs Somersham.'

'Blackmail?' cried the gardener. 'What is he talking of, Mother? Tell him you know not what he means! Mr Holmes, we only didn't tell of our relations because Mother said she had heard that the Duke frowned upon such arrangements amongst the staff. He felt it could interfere with the operation of the household.'

'I say, Holmes!' Lord Freddie, who had maintained a stiff silence in the corner of the room, could conceal his exasperation no longer. 'What the deuce does this have to do with father's condition?'

'Everything. It is the cause of his collapse and retreat. Lord Freddie, have you met this gardener before?'

'No, I don't think so.'

Holmes looked at his friend and said gently, 'In that case, let me introduce you to your brother.'

Both men stared at each other, then at Holmes, at me and finally at the cook, who looked as if she might faint. Holmes took her by the arm and steered her to a chair.

'Holmes! You go too far! Explain yourself this instant!' The confusion upon His Lordship's face was mixed with astonishment and perplexity. It was at that point that I first noticed the physical similarity between Lord Freddie and the gardener.

'Very well. Westbridge – or rather Somersham – is your half-brother. He is the result of an indiscretion on the Duke's part some thirty-eight years ago. You will note that that makes him one year older than you. His mother, having been supported by the Duke all these years, finally determined to wring what last she could from him. To that end, she secured positions for herself and her son here at Bagshot Hall. The Duke saw them talking in the garden on the afternoon he was taken ill. He realised what it meant, of course. He suspected his secret would soon be exposed, and so his breakdown was accompanied by a retreat to his chamber. He would not venture into the garden. His paranoia grew quickly and he became convinced that Mrs Somersham might try to poison him as an act of vengeance. What was it you asked of him, madam?'

13

'I just wanted my boy to take his rightful position,' she nodded at her son. 'My lad was the first born. This house and the title should be his.'

Her son's visage showed his confusion and disbelief. 'I didn't know! I didn't know, sir! Truly, sir, I was not aware of this preposterous story.'

I instinctively felt that the gardener was honest.

Holmes looked at him for a few seconds. 'I know you are telling the truth, Somersham. I believe you and your brother to be the only innocent parties in this débâcle. As for you, madam, what did you have on the Duke? Letters, was it?'

The cook nodded silently.

'They must be returned at once,' Holmes said severely. 'His Grace has agreed that he will continue to take care of your financial requirements for as long as you live. He will, in fact, establish a fund to ensure that you and your family want for nothing even should he pass away. In return, he expects total discretion and privacy. You must know that your son would have difficulty in establishing a strong claim, despite his superior age.'

The gardener had regained his composure and spoke in a calm yet penetrating tone. 'I have no wish for his position.' He indicated Lord Frederic. 'I was not brought up for it. I know nothing of affairs of state or the world he lives in. I have a girl, an honest, kindly and wonderful girl, who has promised to be mine. She would not want me any other way.'

Lord Freddie gazed intently at his brother then he strode across and clasped his hand.

Holmes immediately walked to the door. Flinging it open, he said, 'Please come in now, Your Grace.' An elderly gentleman with a lined but not unkindly expression entered and walked slowly toward us.

'I think we are about done here, Watson,' Holmes whispered to me. Quietly we made our retreat and headed for the local hostelry, where comfortable rooms were made available to us for the night.

*****

It was only when we were back in Baker Street the next morning that Holmes indicated that he was ready to explain the entire circumstances of the previous day's revelations. I sat enjoying my first cigar of the day, while Holmes reached for the Persian slipper and kneaded the rough tobacco that was his preference into one of his oldest and foulest briars.

'It was a simple affair. Indeed, I had most of the information at hand before we left this room. I was able to recall several similar cases, although the source of the blackmail was novel in this instance. I immediately determined that the cause of the Duke's reaction was in the garden where he walked. What could that source be but a person? The fact that he then retired to his chambers and refused sustenance from his own kitchens indicated a fear of poisoning. So, we arrive at the conclusion that it must be a member of his staff of whom he was afraid. That this reaction occurred recently suggested that it must be staff appointed while his son was away. Lord Freddie described a curse upon his family. I felt confident in dismissing such a notion, but he also mentioned a previous Duke who had, by his irascible ways, fallen into a mire of scandal.

'I concluded that the shock must be truly great for a vigorous and robust man such as the Duke to suffer such a rapid decline. What greater fear could such a man have but disgrace, dishonour and public scandal? The fact that it seemed related to his staff suggested that age-old weakness of certain members of the aristocracy.'

Holmes looked at me and sighed. 'I decided that the most likely scenario was that he had seen a former conquest with her offspring – an offspring who could, should the truth out, threaten the very accession of his existing son and heir.

'When I entered the Duke's chambers I was at first received with little warmth. His Grace perceived me as a troublemaker and a meddler. It was not the first time that I have been accused of such traits, as you well know.' Holmes allowed himself a wry chuckle. 'I was able to reassure the Duke that my intentions were only to ease his burden, and I reminded him how his son and I were acquainted. He immediately recalled the circumstances and warmed to me. As I was already in possession of most of the facts, I recounted what I knew and His Grace filled in a couple of the minor details.

'Upon returning to the drawing-room, I knew that I was looking for an older woman and a younger man. As you know, I have made a study of human facial physiognomy so it was not difficult to perceive the man who bore features in common with the Duke and Lord Freddie. He also possessed characteristics of his mother, the cook. The resulting developments you saw for yourself.'

'But Holmes, if you will permit me – and I certainly would never wish to pry – how did you and Lord Freddie become so intimately acquainted?' I felt that unless I could secure an answer I would be cheated.

Holmes smiled. 'More than twenty years ago, a young and rather foolhardy youth chose to spend his weekends climbing cliffs around the southern coastline of our fair isle. Upon one occasion he rather overstretched his abilities and fell some thirty or more feet onto a ledge where he lay in agony, his arm bent at a most grotesque angle. It was sheer happenstance that he was found. Despite considerable personal danger, his rescuer climbed down to him and secured his recovery. His saviour, being a man of modesty, related the tale to few and saved the young man's blushes.'

'I say, Holmes, that was a fine introduction! The Duke must be indebted to you for saving his son from so foolhardy an exploit.'

Holmes laughed aloud, a rarity in itself. 'No, my dear Watson, I fear you have it the wrong way around.'

*****

As a postscript, I should mention a letter that Holmes received some weeks later. It was on the same tea-scented paper as before. He read it attentively and passed it to me. I must say I was much moved by its contents. Lord Frederic expressed his thanks for both Holmes' work and his new brother.

My friend expressed no surprise. 'That is the measure of the man, Watson. I expected nothing less,' were his final words on the matter.

The Case of the Ancient Artefact

Our footsteps echoed loudly as Holmes and I strode the long marble-floored corridors of the British Museum. We were preceded by the hurrying figure of the Curator of Antiquities as we passed treasure after treasure with barely a glance. It was August of 1888, and the heat of our sun was baking the capital with a relentless ferocity that made even me, who had served in India and Afghanistan, begin to weary of its assault.

The delicious coolness of the capacious building was therefore most pleasant and welcome. My companion often seemed impervious to the vagaries of our climate, his countenance rarely betraying the effects of either heat or cold. While I confess my collar was providing me with considerable discomfort, Holmes, by contrast, appeared composed and purposeful as ever.

Without warning, we entered the gallery of Africa and there, in front of a glass case in the very centre of the vast room, we stopped. Broken glass crunched under our leather soles and Holmes held up a cautioning hand.

'Who has been here?' His voice was sharp.

'The police, sir,' replied Mapplewhite, our host. 'They were here until not twenty minutes ago.'

Holmes drew a deep breath and I knew he was steeling himself for how much crucial evidence might have already been corrupted or destroyed. 'Gentlemen, would you be so kind as to retire to the doorway while I make some observations.' It was not asked in the manner of a question.

Mapplewhite and I carefully retraced our steps and stood quietly while Holmes circumnavigated the great gallery. Occasionally he paused as if in deep thought then, suddenly invigorated, he seemed to fly about the room, one moment scrabbling on top of a dark mahogany table, the next on his very knees peering through his lens at the joints in the marble floor.

Mapplewhite caught my eye and raised a questioning eyebrow, but I knew my friend of old and simply raised my finger to my lips, giving the anxious curator what I hoped was a reassuring smile.

'I have been able to discern only a couple of salient facts, gentlemen,' said the great detective a few minutes later. 'There is very little here upon which to remark. I take it neither you, nor your staff or the police could find any signs of forced entry to the windows?'

Mapplewhite confirmed that this was the case.

'Further, nothing else is missing?' enquired my friend as if he already knew the answer.

'Why yes, sir! There were two small figurines in the gallery next door but they are worth so little by comparison to the magnificent statue that I am surprised the thief was interested in them. Perhaps he took them on impulse, or just liked the look of them.'

'Of course, that must be it,' said Holmes dismissively. 'There is nothing else for me to observe here. Pray show me where the figures were placed.'

A few strides saw our little band standing in front of a large cabinet, its glass display door ajar. Holmes spent considerable time examining the lock and fine mahogany edging to the doors with the large magnifying lens that was as much a part of his personal attire as a dog collar is to a priest or a pocket watch to a station master.

It was not until more than ten minutes had elapsed that he pronounced himself satisfied, straightened up and turned to the expectant curator. 'Tell me, Mr Mapplewhite, could you put a value on the stolen artefacts?'

'It is very difficult, sir. A piece such as this statue comes up for sale so rarely and is – was,' he corrected himself, 'almost beyond compare. I should think it would have a financial value of not less than £50,000.'

'Great Heavens!' I heard myself exclaim.

Holmes shot me a glance. 'And the figurines?'

21

'Perhaps a hundred or two at most, and then only to the most particular of collectors.'

'I see. I take it that you have photographs or drawings of all the pieces in your catalogues?'

'Of course. I have them in my office.'

'Then let us retire there, where you may familiarise me further with the missing items,' said Holmes. He immediately began to move off in pursuit of the curator who, while short of stature, seemed to possess a disproportionately rapid means of locomotion, doubtless a result of many years traversing the long galleries of his workplace.

Not many minutes passed before we were both ensconced in comfortable leather tub chairs and tea was being poured in our host's comfortable sitting room. My gaze swept the many shelves and bookcases and I was impressed by a number of fine paintings and curios from the four corners of our Earth, but Holmes, as was his manner, was entirely business. At his instruction, the hapless guardian of some of the nation's greatest treasures began his story.

'The missing statue is made from the highest quality marble, inlaid and encrusted with precious and semi-precious gemstones. Very little is known of its origin, and indeed its age, save that it was recovered in Africa and is thought by some to be evidence of a highly skilled civilisation that existed several millennia ago. I am not convinced of this; the craftsmanship is so far advanced compared with what the natives of that great continent can achieve today that I struggle to accept that they could have regressed to such an extent. The piece is thought to be a model of a king or a god, but we have no other example that bears any resemblance to it in our collection, nor to my knowledge does any other museum in this country or overseas. Indeed, I have remarked on several occasions that I am not convinced that it is African at all, but it is in the African collection because the first recording we have of it was from the Earl of Sutherland, who obtained it from a dubious source in Morocco in the early years of this century.'

Our host paused, withdrew a foolscap folder from a case beside the table, and passed across several images. 'We are in the process of photographing all the most important items in our collections,' he offered by way of explanation. 'So these are recent and of high quality.'

Holmes studied the large-format photographs carefully. 'A magnificent piece, without a doubt. Even in monochrome, it is undoubtedly impressive. No doubt it is very heavy?' He passed the plate over to me and I gazed at a remarkable figure of a man, his hands reaching out as if in welcome, with a face that was neither Caucasian nor Negroid.

'Heavy?' replied the curator. 'Why, yes, I suppose it is indeed of considerable weight. I myself should not wish to carry it a great distance.'

'And the small figurines?' Holmes asked.

'I have copies of the plates made of them here, but I'm afraid they are not of the same quality as the images of the statue.' He passed across two smaller and less-defined images of a pair of oddly proportioned and quite rudimentary figures, one obviously male and the other female. Holmes studied the pictures intently then abruptly stood and bade us follow him.

This time it was Mapplewhite and I who found ourselves hurrying to keep up as Holmes strode back to the African Gallery. There he found a small door to a tradesman's alley discreetly hidden in the corner of the large room. He flung open the door onto a small passage with many old crates and sacks stacked to one side. My colleague wasted no time in pulling the detritus aside, prodding and poking until, with an exultant cry, he ceased his foraging. 'Would you be so good as to step over here a moment?' he requested of the bemused curator.

Craning forward, I could scarcely have been more amazed than to see Holmes cast aside an old tarpaulin to reveal the missing statue.

Mapplewhite gasped, 'How on God's earth…? I simply can't believe it! Mr Holmes, your formidable reputation doesn't do you justice, sir!' Reverently he picked up the heavy statue and cradled it gently.

We returned to the gallery. A porter was quickly sent for and the precious trophy taken into safe custody.

'And now,' said my colleague, 'we must repair to the good curator's office once more and discuss the real mystery.' With those words, the eminent detective swung on his heel and strode off in the direction of the snug.

Once we were seated again, Holmes carefully retrieved the pictures of the two small figurines. He composed himself and began to speak in a low tone. 'You claim these artefacts are of minor interest and unremarkable. I disagree.' He held up the prints. 'They are undoubtedly of great significance and of considerably greater import to the thief than the statue. Indeed, the taking of the statue was merely intended to divert our attention and confound our enquiries for a time. These diminutive icons are what the thief – or thieves – were intent upon procuring.'

The curator was staring at my friend open mouthed. 'How can you possibly determine all this? I'll admit I was amazed by your recovery of the statue, but surely the thief hid it there because he was startled and intended to return to collect it later.'

'Nonsense,' replied Holmes firmly. 'The case the statue resided in was smashed in a haphazard fashion. No care or attention was given to the item inside. It was done quickly and as an afterthought. By contrast, the display cabinet in which the two figurines resided was carefully lock picked. The thief went to great pains to ensure that no damage was rendered to the exhibits within. He would not have taken such care if he had simply decided to snatch the items as an afterthought.

'Once I had deduced this, it appeared increasingly likely that the thief would not labour to escape carrying a heavy and bulky item when all he truly needed was a duffel bag in which to transport his real prize. Therefore, it seemed obvious that he would have hidden it locally. It was,' Holmes lowered his voice in admiration, 'a very clever move. You and the police would chase after the statue for a day or so until it was discovered during a more thorough search. All parties would be so pleased to have recovered the valuable item that they would probably agree to let the minor items pass. Am I not correct?'

Mapplewhite agreed. 'What you say is most likely true. I would have been happy enough at the recovery of the statue. But you have raised more questions than you have answered, Mr Holmes. I cannot now dismiss the figurines. We must determine why they are so valuable and work tirelessly until they are recovered.'

'Indeed. You should devote your time to gathering as much information concerning the missing figures as is necessary. I require all the known facts regarding these remarkable exhibits to be collated and passed to me at the earliest opportunity. In particular, I wish to know where they may have been procured and by whom, and any other matters of interest even if conjecture or hearsay. In the meantime, I shall make some enquiries of my own. Perhaps we might agree to reconvene here at noon tomorrow? Good day!'

*****

Twice during our journey back to Baker Street Holmes bade the driver stop. Each time, without explanation, he leapt from our hansom and disappeared into a side street or alleyway for perhaps five minutes before returning and settling wordlessly into his seat once more.

It was not until we were back in our rooms, and Mrs Hudson had delivered a great earthenware jug of cooling lemonade, that my friend met my gaze. 'This is a delicate case, Watson. Time is of the very essence.'

I agreed vigorously and offered the opinion that if the figurines were not recovered soon, they might never be seen again. Holmes appeared distracted, and gazed absently out of the window. 'What? Oh no, Watson, I'm very sure that they will re-surface in a year or less. But most probably they will be far beyond our reach by then.'

Even I was surprised by his certainty. My thoughts were that the items would be winging their way at this very minute toward the locked cabinets of a wealthy private collector, and they would rarely see the light of day again.

Holmes continued, 'The key is in their origin. If we know from whence they came, perhaps we can determine their significance. Still, we can do nothing until the thief makes himself known to us, so I suggest a light supper of some of Mrs Hudson's excellent gammon and pickle sandwiches while we await developments.'

Holmes reached for the Persian slipper and busied himself with packing a substantial briar.

*****

It was not until a quarter past eight, when the heat of the day had settled into a balmy evening and Holmes and I were halfway through our second cigars, that there came a knock at the door and Mrs Hudson entered.

'A gentleman to see you, Mr Holmes.' Her look of disapproval did not go unnoticed as she ushered in a small man dressed in simple, though not dowdy, clothes. He stepped lightly as he glanced about our room.

Holmes waved him to a chair and waited until our good housekeeper had closed the door behind her. 'So it was you, Simpkins. I thought as much,' he said coolly.

Our guest stared us both squarely in the eyes before giving a non-committal shrug. I detected considerable intelligence in the man and a certain quiet assuredness that was not typical of his apparent class.

'Watson, let me introduce you to Charlie Simpkins, one of the foremost thieves in our great city, perhaps in the entire country.'

'I received your message Mr 'Olmes. I'm not saying I did it or didn't do it, but I'll listen to what you have to say.'

'I suggest you do listen and attend to my words very carefully, Simpkins. I require your co-operation in the recovery of two items removed from the British Museum yesterday without the permission of the curators of the aforesaid institution. In this instance, should I receive information useful to me in my enquiries, I may be inclined to spend little energy in the apprehension of the person who took the items and instead focus my resources on the recovery and restoration of the items.'

Simpkins regarded the detective carefully. His clear blue eyes never wavered as he weighed up his options and considered his predicament.

Holmes continued, steel entering his voice. 'However, if I should not receive such co-operation, I will, as my note suggested, not rest until the thief is hunted down, tried and sentenced to spend the next several years at Her Majesty's pleasure. You must know, Simpkins, that I will be as good as my word, and that I am a formidable foe.'

Our guest's mind appeared made up. With a small sigh, he shrugged his shoulders again, this time in resignation. 'I will help you all I can. After all, I care not what happens to the items but I do care about my liberty. If I have your word that you will overlook my involvement, then I will furnish you with the facts as I know them.'

'No, I will give no such assurance. If matters unravel as to show you in a most unfavourable light, or if my investigations suggest a deeper and more sinister involvement on your part, then you may be certain that I will never hesitate in ensuring that you face the full weight of British justice. If, though, your involvement is simply one of a hired hand and you are completely candid with me, as I have indicated I will not make any particular efforts in your direction.'

Simpkins frowned then said, 'Well, you really give me no choice, Mr Sherlock Holmes. I will tell you what I know, which anyways isn't much, I can promise you.'

Holmes settled back in his chair and closed his eyes. 'Proceed,' he said quietly.

'Well, sir, as you know I have certain abilities that can be of use whenever a person requires the recovery of a certain item from a difficult location. I am selective in who I work for, and I have never employed violence or inflicted personal harm in any of my work. I am, I believe, recognised as a leading practitioner in my field and therefore I am sought out and commissioned on occasion.

'It was about a fortnight past when I received word that a certain gentleman was interested in utilising my skills and I agreed to meet with him to discuss his requirements.'

'How did you receive word? Where did you meet? When and what time?' Holmes asked curtly.

'I heard through my acquaintances – well, the landlord of the Blacksmith's Arms, if the truth be told. We met on the Embankment by the Needle at eleven o'clock at night. That would have been on Wednesday last. The seventeenth, it was.'

'Describe the gentleman you met. Be careful to be accurate and give a full account.'

'He was not tall, perhaps not more than five and a half feet. He was wrapped in a cloak, which appeared unusual given the time of the year. I barely saw his face as he kept it away from me and out of the light from the new electric lamps. I did get the strong impression that he was very dark-skinned, with almost impossibly white teeth and eyes.'

'His voice?'

'That of a softly spoken gentleman, sir. I could not perceive any accent.'

'And the commission?'

Simpkins hesitated.

'Now don't be foolish. Tell me what I ask,' commanded Holmes.

'A thousand pounds, Mr 'Olmes.'

Somewhat astonished, I whistled softly at the burglar's revelation.

A small smile spread across Holmes' face. 'Thank you, Simpkins. You may go now. If I have need for you again I will send for you. In that eventuality, I shall expect you to respond instantly.'

After the thief had left, I rounded on Holmes. 'I am astounded! You are going to let that man get away with his crime. You realise that makes us a party to a felony!'

'My dear Watson, I have no doubt that my path will cross Simpkins' again, and that the outcome will be quite different. In this instance, he is but a pawn in a much larger and more significant game. I have allowed a smaller fish to go free in order that I might set my line for the greater prize.'

My frown must have conveyed my doubts, for Holmes spoke his exasperation. 'Really, Watson, sometimes my methods may be less than savoury but I am not the police, nor is my service retained by them. Further, it is not my place to make up for their deficiency so I must apply my own judgment as to the greater good.'

Reluctantly, I nodded my agreement. 'So was his information worth the price of his liberty?'

'Oh yes. He has been most illuminating. My suspicions have been largely confirmed, although I do not yet know the location of the missing items nor the identity of the crime's commissioner. However, I am still confident that I will be able to discern the true facts of the matter before noon tomorrow.'

Familiar as I was with my friend's unorthodox methods, I could only assume that Holmes already had a suspect in mind. When I put it to him, he denied it and replied, 'Not a suspect precisely. I will need to make further enquiries before I can draw any conclusions. I must now venture out for an hour and a half. Upon my return, we shall dine at Mapleson's where I understand the fillet of beef is exceptionally good this week.'

*****

The beef was indeed excellent and we were savouring our cigars when a messenger arrived and discreetly passed Holmes a folded note. After quickly reading it, my companion passed it across to me. I read that Mapplewhite had narrowed the country of origin to one of three.

While I was digesting the content of the missive, Holmes pulled a card from his pocket and scribbled a note, which he gave the messenger who departed at speed. I was almost beside myself with curiosity but knew from experience that Holmes enjoyed his little drama and would only take me into his confidence at exactly the point he deemed conducive to a successful outcome.

The detective took a deep sip from his brandy balloon and stood up, gesturing for his coat and the bill in one movement. 'Come, Watson. I think this evening is about to become most interesting.'

*****

Some quarter of an hour later, Holmes and I found ourselves strolling along the marvellous Victoria

Embankment. I recall how the night air was refreshing and pleasing; even Holmes remarked upon it and seemed quite content to amble along at a relaxed pace until presently we approached Cleopatra's Needle. I became aware that a darkly clothed figure was already there and appeared to stiffen at our approach.

'Good evening, sir,' spoke Holmes as we gained upon him. 'It is a most pleasant night; don't you agree?'

'It most certainly is,' replied the figure in a deep and sonorous voice.

Holmes continued on his way, never breaking his stride as I followed at his side. Within a minute or so we rounded a corner and Holmes was immediately the man of action. He hailed a cab and bade the driver make best speed to our rooms, where I was astonished to find Sherlock's corpulent and masterful brother, Mycroft, waiting for us.

'My dear Sherlock, you have bested my operative back here!' Even as he spoke those words, footfalls could be heard upon the stair. Moments later Mrs Hudson presented a most nondescript man whose features were so bland that I struggle to recall them as I write this, save for the fact that he had fair hair. Mycroft and he exchanged a few words before our fair-haired friend departed with no more than a nod toward Holmes and me.

'Well, well, dear brother, you were almost correct. It was not your most likely pick of the three, but indeed it was the Gibeon chargé d'affaires that you greeted not half an hour ago. Your second choice has proved to be the right one.' Mycroft sighed. 'This has now become a most delicate and unfortunate matter. Her Majesty's Government and the Gibeon ruling council have been in difficult discussions for some years now. It is imperative that these talks, which have a wider strategic significance with particular reference to the Boer situation, do not fail at this advanced stage. I must confess I am surprised at this turn of events and I urge you, Sherlock, to treat this matter with the utmost tact and diplomacy. Further, as an independent operative your involvement must remain unofficial. You are acting on behalf of the British Museum and no one else. Are you clear on that most critical point?'

Holmes nodded thoughtfully. 'I am indeed clear, but I assume that recovery of these items is permitted by reasonable means?'

'It is, but there must be no scandal or embarrassment to either side. A theft of a national treasures by an impudent foreign power cannot be tolerated, and all efforts must be made to secure the recovery of such items. However, no purpose will be furthered by the failure of current negotiations.' Then, in a rare display of emotion that might almost have approximated tenderness, Mycroft added, 'I have the utmost faith in you as always, dear brother.'

My friend met his gaze and replied evenly, 'You may be sure that I will bring all my powers and sensibilities to bear on this matter.'

When Mycroft had left, Holmes sat silently in deep contemplation, smoke curling from a briar, his knees drawn up to his chest. I waited quietly, reading a gazette and listening to the clock strike its progress through the closeness of the warm night.

I am not a little embarrassed to say I must have fallen under sleep's intoxicating spell, for when I awoke at three in the morning Holmes was gone. He had left a small note by my sleeve which read: 'Join me for breakfast at Mortimer's. Nine sharp.'

*****

I found Holmes already seated at our favourite table in the famous restaurant. He appeared relaxed and bright-eyed. 'Watson! Try the cinnamon toast, it really is rather good.'

We steadily ate our way through a splendid repast, Holmes displaying a heartier appetite than was his usual custom. When we had finished, Holmes declared that we had an appointment to keep and should not be tardy.

I was surprised when our cab drew up outside an unprepossessing building just off St James's Square. A small, plain, brass plaque by the door proclaimed the building to be the Embassy of Gibeon but, with that exception, the house was unremarkable in all its features.

Holmes made use of the heavy gilt door knocker and presently we were shown inside by an immaculately dressed servant, resplendent in spotless whites and gaiters. We were propelled down a corridor and shown into an expensively appointed office. The servant presented us both to the ambassador and retired, quietly closing the heavy oak door behind him as he left.

The ambassador was a large and tastefully dressed black man who spoke with a thick accent. He was obviously accustomed to wielding authority as he waved us both to comfortable armchairs. 'Mr Holmes, I understand that you are an independent agent of the law. Please can you inform me as to your interest in my government and my country?'

'Your Excellency, I must assure you that my interest is only as a result of a small matter that is of little consequence. I wish only to save any unfortunate embarrassment on all sides. You may be unaware that two nights ago there was a theft of two small figurines from the British Museum...'

A troubled look passed across the ambassador's face. 'But you surely don't mean to suggest that the Gibeon Government has any involvement in such a matter?' Although polite, there was no mistaking the warning in the man's tone.

'I suggest nothing at present, sir. I am merely exploring a number of avenues of enquiry, of which this is but one. I can offer my further assurance that it is my desire to conclude the matter rapidly and with the minimum of public knowledge. Discretion is in the interests of both your government and mine.'

'You did not say that you represent the British government in this matter, Mr Holmes.' The ambassador was undoubtedly a shrewd man.

'You are correct, sir, I did not say that,' countered my friend. 'However, you may be sure that significant public figures are taking a keen interest in the progression of this case.' Holmes paused in order for his words to achieve their full weight and significance.

The ambassador sighed heavily. 'So how am I to be of help in the recovery of these figurines, Mr Holmes?'

'I wish you to do nothing, precisely nothing, between the hours of eight and nine o'clock this evening. I require you to remain here at the embassy in this very study. I shall send word to you soon after that hour. But before I take my leave, I would very much like to have a look at your roof. Would you be so kind as to show me upstairs? In the meantime, Watson, I would be grateful if you might make a most thorough inspection of the gardens and note any features of interest. Please pay particular attention to any entry and exit points, and the flowers that grow in the beds.'

*****

Perhaps twenty minutes later Holmes and I were once again in a cab heading toward the British Museum where our adventures had begun not twenty-four hours previously. I began to brief Holmes on my findings, only to become rapidly disenchanted as he appeared entirely uninterested. He waved my report away and continued to stare vacantly at the passing façades as our cab tripped over the cobbles. With no small degree of annoyance, I settled back into my seat and quietly bridled with indignation until we arrived at the great edifice.

As we alighted and were about to begin our ascent of the steps at the grand entrance, I could contain my irritation no longer. 'I must say, Holmes, I think its jolly poor form of you to set me a task and then display complete contempt for my endeavours.'

Holmes was suddenly at his most charming, 'My dear Watson, please forgive me. I needed you to divert the attention of the staff and to give the impression that my investigations were of a more general nature. I must say that you performed your assignment admirably and your antics gained much attention from them. I too observed with pleasure your singularly enthusiastic assault upon the garden wall.'

Although I considered I should have remained dissatisfied, my friend's occasional winning smile was most disarming and I began to see the humour in the situation. Indeed, I stifled a laugh as I mounted the steps in pursuit of Holmes, who bounded up them two at a time.

Before I had time to question my companion further, Mapplewhite, the curator of African Antiquities, arrived and ushered us once more toward his office. 'Well, Mr Holmes, have you made any progress?' he asked eagerly as the door closed behind us.

'Perhaps,' replied Holmes with a shrug. 'I am confident that the artefacts have not yet left the country. I am also very sure that excellent care has been taken of them and further, I am still confident of their recovery. But first, Mr Mapplewhite, I would be most interested to hear of your own enquiries.'

'Indeed, Mr Holmes. I have spent some considerable time piecing together what little information we have as to their origins. I should tell you that, other than the fact they are indeed African and probably from the south west of that great continent, I have been able to secure few reliable facts.

'It would seem that they came into the museum's collection some fifty or more years ago. They were donated from the collection of the late Thomas James Brudenell, 7th Earl of Winchester, who, as you know, was later intrinsically involved in the disastrous Charge of the Light Brigade. He procured many items of interest during his time spent in darkest Africa and amongst its peoples.

'It is clear that he came upon them during his travels and I am prepared to make a professional guess that it was during his time in south-western Africa that they were added to his collection.'

'Almost certainly it was during his time in Gibeon, wouldn't you say, Curator?' Holmes threw the comment out as if it was of little consequence.

'Why yes, Mr Holmes, I believe you to be correct! I am most surprised that you have already come to similar conclusions as myself, although I would hazard by very different means.'

'A final question, Mr Mapplewhite. Have you found any indication in your researches that suggests the items are of any particular special value or significance?'

'No, sir. They are certainly ancient, and without doubt interesting curiosities, but I have not been able to determine anything especially remarkable about them. They were put on display as part of a wider exhibition of early African art and they have not been in the public view for many years. As a matter of fact, both idols have remained in store until these past two months.'

Holmes smiled quickly. 'Thank you, Mr Mapplewhite. That is most significant. I may be able to furnish you with a more detailed professional summary of this case tomorrow morning.' And with that Holmes and I departed for Baker Street, yet we were once again not to complete the journey together, for Holmes ordered the cab driver to pause en route and alighted with a cheery, 'Ask Mrs Hudson to provide a hearty tea, there's a good chap. I shall rejoin you within the hour.'

*****

Holmes and I enjoyed an excellent high tea, certainly one of our housekeeper's most sterling efforts. After two cigars, it was at eight o'clock that I heard footfalls on our stairs. Within moments Mrs Hudson had presented an expensively attired black man who stared silently at us before his gaze settled upon my friend.

'Mr Sherlock Holmes, I presume?' He spoke with a deep and cultured English accent. The man was plainly educated in this country, his manner and bearing suggesting he had attended our finer schools and universities.

'Indeed I am he, Your Highness.' Holmes waved the man to a chair. 'I am most gratified you could join us. Watson, may I present to you Prince Mbali Kewatsami, third son of High Chief Kewatsami of the Ruling Council of Gibeon.'

I nodded, trying not to betray my surprise. The young man – I would have put him at no more than five-and-twenty years of age – sat neatly in an easy chair and propped a gold-crested cane against the arm. Leaning forward slightly, he regarded us with his large clear eyes and asked coolly, 'May I be informed as to why you have asked me here, Mr Holmes?'

Holmes smiled, then his face turned stern. 'Oh sir, that really won't do. You must know exactly why I have summoned you.' Our guest moved as if to protest but Holmes held up a hand and continued. 'Please, don't insult me by assuming a pretence of ignorance. I, in turn, will not insult you by assuming you to be a petty thief.'

The Prince didn't flinch for a moment. His eyes shone in the gaslight as he considered his position. Finally, he said, 'My father and my country had nothing to do with it.'

Holmes smiled briefly. 'I am aware of that. What I wish to know is why.'

'Then I shall tell you. Mr Holmes, Dr Watson, my country is an ancient land with many primitive beliefs and customs. My people are comprised of two main tribes, who have warred and fought in the past but now co-exist with some degree of peace. My father has brought his people together.' The pride in his voice was obvious. 'The figurines that were on display in the British Museum are of enormous significance to my country. They were stolen more than half a century ago by a British colonialist, Thomas Brudenell, the 7th Earl of Winchester.'

I must admit I bristled to hear the character of one of my country's most revered heroes denigrated in such a manner. I was about to say as much but Holmes waved me to silence. 'Pray continue.' The detective leaned back in his chair, his eyes narrowed and a look of serenity upon his countenance. I had observed before that Holmes often adopted such an air when he knew he had succeeded and had reached the finale to a case.

'When the museum opened its African exhibition, I was invited to the inaugural reception. You cannot imagine my emotion when I found myself standing before the figurines that I was sure were the missing idols my countrymen have searched for these many years. I knew that I had to ensure that they were returned to their rightful place. They have no financial value outside my country, but their cultural significance to my people is incalculable.'

'But these items are now the property of the British Museum,' ventured Holmes.

'No sir, they are not. They are the property of the Gibeon nation of south-western Africa.' The assuredness and resolve in our guest's voice left us in no doubt as to his certainty on the matter.

'Why did your father not request their return?' countered Holmes.

'He is a proud man, but he is also a pragmatic one. I am not aware of the British Museum returning any items upon request, Mr Holmes. If I had asked, it would have surely indicated my people's interest in this matter and thus made any further attempt to secure them much more problematic. I decided that there was no alternative but to recover them in a clandestine manner.' I detected no trace of remorse or shame in his steady voice.

Holmes sighed. 'This is very difficult, Your Highness. Your ill-considered actions could cause considerable difficulty between our countries at a time when our two governments are working toward a new era of understanding. I must ask you to return the figurines immediately.'

The young man shook his head slowly. 'I cannot comply Mr Holmes. If I were to do so I would betray my people, and for what? So two more artefacts can be placed in a display case and glanced at by spectators who have no understanding of their true significance? No! I cannot do that Mr Holmes. You must do what you will, but I will remain resolute.'

Holmes sighed and reached across to ring for Mrs Hudson. 'I think we are all in need of some refreshment.' Within a few minutes our housekeeper shuffled in bearing a tray laden with crockery and covered by a cloth, which she placed on the small table between us.'

'Thank you, Mrs Hudson. I trust you have provided some of your most excellent cake?'

'Oh yes, Mr Holmes. It was delivered as you requested and is there under the napkin.'

Holmes turned to our guest. 'Will you have some tea, Your Highness?' Holmes' voice was suddenly light and carefree as if we had just been discussing the weather or the latest cricket scores.

'Thank you but no, Mr Holmes. I find myself neither thirsty nor hungry. I must enquire as to your course of action.'

'This cake is most excellent,' continued Holmes as if he had not heard. 'I truly think you should try some...' And with a flourish, the great detective removed the cloth to reveal two small dark carved-wood figurines.

The Prince gasped, his eyes flashing with anger. I felt myself stiffen and readied myself in case I should need to repel a physical assault, but within moments he had regained his composure. 'I see you have the better of me, Mr Holmes. I don't know how you have achieved this feat, but there is no doubt that you are a clever and resourceful man who has served his country well.'

'And I see that you serve yours with dedication and resolve,' replied Holmes courteously. 'I would be most grateful if you could explain the significance of these two figures. The curator at the British Museum and other academics have been able to shed little light upon them. I would like to be able to explain to them the real value of the discovery.'

'Very well. I will tell you the story of those idols and you will see how they are of great import to my people and of little value to anyone else.'

The young prince began his story and I listened in rapt attention. I have always found geographical and cultural matters to be exceptionally interesting, and I was fascinated by such an insight into the early history of the land of his birth.

'Many centuries ago my people were comprised of small bands of wandering families. They held a fundamental allegiance to either the Usawi or M'bengi tribes but spent most of their lives herding their cattle and corralling their goats. My country is a rich and fertile land in part, and some of the Usawi began to settle and cultivate the arable land. Many years passed and the two tribes continued to live much as they had for generations, the Usawi as farmers and the M'bengi as cattle and livestock herders. There would be the occasional skirmish over grazing land or some other trivial matter but, for the most part, both tribes co-existed peaceably enough and traded their wares as benefited them both.

'And then one year there was very little rain in the Usawi uplands. The rivers ran dry and many crops failed. The Usawi, who had by then been farmers for generations, began to starve. They prayed to the gods for rain but none came. Eventually they were forced to leave their land and begin a journey into the heartlands of the M'Bengi. Inevitably there was conflict, followed by many years of war between the tribes as both struggled to survive.

'But slowly the rains returned and the Usawi found that their ancient land had become fertile once again. They returned and began to farm once more. For a dozen years there was peace in the region, but then a drought in the lowlands forced the M'Bengi to move their animals closer and closer to Usawi land. This time the tribal chiefs were wise and weary of war. They met and it was agreed that no

45

more would there be conflict between their peoples. In times of drought and hardship, Usawi would help M'Bengi and M'Bengi would come to the aid of Usawi.

'Two figures were carved to seal this agreement, one by each tribe. They were to represent the unending union between the two peoples, and they were kept in a specially constructed shrine on the border between the two tribal lands as a reminder that in time of need they were forever brother and sister.

'Thus they remained as a symbol of this unity for countless generations, until they were plundered as artefacts and removed to this great capital.' The Prince paused and drew a deep breath. 'You know the rest, Mr Holmes and Dr Watson. My only regret is that I have failed my people in this matter. I will, of course, accept whatever judgement you make as to my personal culpability.'

Holmes was silent for several long moments, then he fixed the young man with a stare and said quietly, 'I do not believe you have failed your people, Your Highness.'

Much to my surprise, my friend turned to me as if we were the only two men in the room. 'Come, Watson. It is a charming evening and I feel we would both benefit from a stroll around Regent's Park and take in some of the cooling air by the boating lake.' With no further comment or acknowledgement of our guest, Holmes led me from our rooms and briskly down the stairs.

'Holmes, I am astounded at your resolution to this matter. You must tell how these two figurines made so dramatic a reappearance on Mrs Hudson's tea tray!' I could hardly contain my astonishment as to how such a seemingly miraculous feat had been accomplished.

'Aha! My good Watson, I see you are consumed by curiosity as always! In order to save your nerves any further unnecessary excitement, I shall explain.

'It was a relatively simple though delicate matter. When we visited the embassy I already knew the likely identity of the individual who had commissioned Simpkins the burglar to procure the figures. I needed to be sure that this was a personal matter and not a governmental one, so I made the Gibeon Ambassador complicit in the recovery of the items as he was evidently aware that public exposure of the thefts would serve his country very badly. He could not sanction the entry and search of the embassy by a foreign national, nor could he conduct the search himself for that would put him in an impossible situation if he found the items.

'As I pretended to study the roof and upper floors in general, I was specifically ascertaining the quarters of our young prince and determining entry and access points. It was most important that the staff of the embassy did not notice my efforts and betray my hand to the royal chargé d'affaires, so I asked you to engage in a thorough examination of the garden in full view of the windows. I knew that my faithful Watson would rise to the occasion and provide a splendid spectacle that would be sure to enthral scullery maid and high official alike.

'I determined the ideal route to gain the prince's rooms and produced a detailed sketch, which I then passed on to Simpkins. The burglar repaid my earlier leniency by performing a special job at my bidding, specifically between the hours of nine and ten, when we were assured that the Prince would be sitting in our rooms at Baker Street.

'Upon recovering the figurines, Simpkins made haste to our lodgings and handed them to the erstwhile Mrs Hudson who had been previously instructed to respond to my questioning about her excellent cake in either the positive or negative, depending upon whether or not Simpkins' mission had met with success. You then bore witness to the final chapter.'

'But Holmes,' I ventured, 'while I could not disagree with the moral claim to the ownership of these idols, I am sure that such a decision was not yours to make.'

Holmes smiled wanly. 'Well then, whose? Some civil servant who has no interest in the matter? The government? We know it would have served no purpose for the state to become involved. Besides,' Holmes winked mischievously, 'I was under strict instructions from the government to avoid public scandal and embarrassment.'

'No, you weren't,' I countered. 'Mycroft asked you to handle the matter delicately and without causing a political incident. It was your brother who asked, not Her Majesty's Government.'

'Aah, but you forget, Watson, that at certain times they are one and the same.'

The Curse of the Purser's Mate

Editor's Note: This account was discovered stamped with the Admiralty 'Top Secret' mark and sealed with the directive that details were not to be released until 1989 under the hundred years' rule. It is printed here in its original form.

On occasion, Mr Sherlock Holmes would be retained by one of the great bastions of British society. Several times my friend had been called upon to engage in clandestine work for Her Majesty's Government and its agents, both in this country and abroad. The deplorable case of the Belgian Ambassador, and how so delicate an outcome Holmes had been forced to weigh, are still vivid in my mind, just as the icy hand that clutches at my heart reminds me of the dreadful consequences had we erred.

However, it was with some surprise that the world's greatest consulting detective received a telegram from Sir James Caddington, Rear-Admiral of the Royal Navy one November morning of the year 1889. Even now, some years later, I shudder to recall the events that made even me, an experienced doctor and veteran of the Indian and Afghan campaigns, recoil in horror at the beastliness of which man is capable. Indeed, it is my intention to lay the facts before the reader without the prejudice and sensationalism that has been made so popular by the penny dreadfuls.

Holmes read the telegram several times but appeared unable to discern much of any interest from it other than the content, so he threw it over to me.

Mr Sherlock Holmes,

Please make haste to meet me at noon today. The matter is most delicate, and time is of the essence. I shall arrange for you to be met from the train and escorted to my office from the 9.23 departing Waterloo.

Yours,

Rear-Admiral Sir James Caddington.

My curiosity was immediately piqued and I could not resist asking Holmes if I might travel with him in order to render any assistance as I might be able and record events as they transpired. Although an army man, I have a fondness and awe for ships, and a foray to Portsmouth at the behest of an admiral was too great a prospect for excitement to ignore.

'Watson, I would be delighted if you were to accompany me and to document this case with care. I have an inclination that it might prove to be most interesting, and not merely as a result of its immediate environs. Regardless, if we are not to disappoint an admiral, we must make haste to Waterloo and catch the 9.23 to Portsmouth. I fear Mrs Hudson's excellent breakfast will have to remain largely unsullied.'

Within minutes a hansom had been summoned and Holmes and I were making rapid progress toward the great station, I with a thick bacon sandwich I had quickly constructed from our abandoned table, and Holmes with an especially strong cigarette firmly clamped between his thin lips.

*****

Portsmouth was, as it had always been, a town with a singular purpose and *raison d'être*. For as long as history had been recorded, ships had been built there and the Royal Navy has operated from its massive docks to repel numerous attempts by foreign powers to inflict injury or invasion upon our fair isle. Indeed, our island nation has enjoyed supremacy of the seas for many centuries and there is no place more intrinsically connected to our maritime prowess than the town into which our train now drew.

No sooner had Holmes and I alighted from our carriage than I perceived two young ratings hustling toward us. I straightened, as I always found myself doing when confronted by other serving men, and favoured them with a smile as they snapped to attention before us.

'Able Seaman Barker, sir,' said the first. 'We have been ordered to escort you to base immediately upon your arrival. Please be so good as to follow us, sirs.'

Holmes arched an eyebrow at me and I perceived he was thinking along similar lines as I: the pace of our summons and the immediacy of our journey seemed to predict a most urgent situation. Unusually, there on the platform in the freezing cold and pouring rain, I found myself feeling a little uneasy. I am not a man given to superstition or nerves but, had I known what lay in store for my friend and I not many hours in the future, I am not entirely sure I would not have turned about tail then and there and returned to Baker Street.

*****

A short carriage ride saw us deposited at the main entrance to the historic dockyards where we found an aide already waiting for us. Not many minutes later, we were ushered into a capacious office lit by massive arched windows overlooking a parade ground and providing views to a grey and forbidding sea beyond.

A tall man was standing motionless gazing out to The Solent, his pristine uniform replete with numerous decorations that became even more apparent as he turned to face us. His eyes, grey and hard, portrayed not only breeding but also immense self-control and discipline. He glanced at our escort who retreated from the room, carefully closing the large carved double oak doors behind him.

Only when we three were alone did the man speak. 'Gentlemen, I am Rear-Admiral Sir James Caddington. I am grateful for your expeditious response to my request.' He motioned to three studded-leather armchairs arranged around a small table on which was placed silver tea and coffee pots and the accompanying fine china crockery.

Holmes and I obeyed his entreaty. Once we had poured our refreshments, our host cleared his throat and addressed us. 'I asked you here against every principle I hold dear. All my military life I have believed that the Senior Service should deal with its matters of discipline, investigate our own transgressions and deal fairly and decisively with those found to have not upheld the standards we expect and require.'

The Rear-Admiral fixed us both with an even gaze. 'I have always believed that this is the correct way for Her Majesty's Navy to conduct its affairs so as to maintain public trust and ensure that our enemies never perceive a weakness in our ranks. My view remains unchanged.'

'Yet you have you summoned us,' observed Holmes quietly and clearly.

'I have requested your presence because we are faced with events unprecedented in the long history of the Royal Navy, and because I fear that only skills such as yours may be able to shed light where today there is only darkness. I have also been assured that, although a civilian, both you and Dr Watson are men of absolute discretion and loyalty to the Crown.'

I nodded vigorously as my companion replied, 'Well then, I hope that your confidence will not prove misplaced. But I must inform you, sir, that I am not a miracle worker. I may be able to help you but first you must furnish me with every fact, no matter how trivial, that you have in your possession.'

'I shall do better than that. I will show you what we discovered yesterday and then I will endeavour to provide you with any further information you may request.'

*****

Our small group, with the Rear-Admiral's aide whose name I learned was Lambert, donned greatcoats and strode the short distance of a few hundred yards from the Admiralty Office to the side of No.3 Dock. There an immense vessel, HMS *Benbow*, lay quietly in the gathering gloom, rain lashing her great superstructure. The *Benbow*, I was to learn later, was one of the newest vessels in the Royal Navy, commissioned only a year previously and built to the most modern design. Not only was she massive, weighing more than ten and a half thousand tons gross and being nearly 350 feet in length, but she was also beautiful in a way that defies an easy explanation. Undoubtedly she exuded power with her huge sixteen-and-a-quarter-inch guns that could be trained through almost 300 degrees due to her barbette configuration, but also the balance of her lines and the clarity of her purpose created a breath-taking sight on such a forbidding day. However, as we approached I became aware of a significant number of armed naval men positioned carefully around the perimeter of the dock.

'I took every precaution to ensure that nothing was disturbed and that no one could embark or disembark the vessel without my knowledge,' the Rear-Admiral informed us.

Holmes voiced his approval and together we ascended to the main deck before departing the freezing salty air and venturing below to one of the numerous storage holds.

At every deck and ladder a guard snapped to attention before standing easy as we passed. I felt a growing unease as we journeyed further into the belly of the ship deep below the waterline. The level of security undoubtedly indicated the gravity of the situation as the Rear-Admiral perceived it; the fact that the ship's guardians carried Martini-Henry rifles confirmed it.

It was not until we had reached a partitioned area of the main quartermaster's stores the Admiral stopped and turned to us. 'The HMS *Benbow* has these last two days returned from an extended patrol of the southern Mediterranean where she has remained for three largely routine months. During that time the vessel ensured safe escort for a number of merchantmen and delivered some papers and materials to our embassy in Morocco. All things considered it was a very uneventful cruise, except for the disappearance of Able Seaman Arthur Coggins during a storm on the night of the thirteenth of October. An investigation was conducted by the captain and his first officer and it was concluded that the aforementioned man had been lost overboard.'

The admiral must have noted my look of concern because he added, 'Life at sea can be hard and not without risk, gentlemen. Loss of men overboard, although much less frequent than it was, is not particularly unusual and an accepted inevitability.'

Holmes interjected, 'So far I see no reason for the presence of Dr Watson and myself, so I conclude that you have not reached the end of your story. I ask you now to keep only to the facts as you know them and present them without prejudice.'

'Very well, Mr Holmes. Two weeks after the loss of Able Seaman Coggins, who fulfilled the duties of purser's mate, the ship's cook had reason to use stores from this very hold in which we now stand. He opened that cask of flour over against the wall.' He gestured toward a stout drum of oak bound with iron hoops. 'As a result of what he found, an immediate search was conducted with the end result being the opening of this barrel.' The Rear-Admiral paused and reached down to remove the lid of the barrel around which we stood.

I am not a man given to a nervous disposition, and I fancy I have seen bloodier sights than most, but I confess I was shocked and repulsed by what I saw within that innocent-looking receptacle. Looking up at us with sightless eyes was the disembodied head of a man who looked to have been not more than twenty-five years of age.

Holmes was silent for a moment before speaking. 'I take it that our unfortunate sailor is still here, in a manner of speaking, in his entirety. What was found in the wall locker, Rear-Admiral?'

'The locker contained an arm and a leg, and the hopper of grain over there held the remaining limbs. The fifty-gallon cask of wine the torso.'

'And all the crew are confined to base?' enquired the detective.

'Indeed they are and have been kept incommunicado. Of course, rumours are running amok already, and I will have to move to address the growing disquiet very soon lest morale begins to suffer more than it has already. At present the men have been told that there is a possibility of contagion from a foreign disease and that they must, therefore, be kept in quarantine for a few days. The cook who made the discovery has been kept separate from the rest of the crew.'

The Rear-Admiral sighed and, for a moment, I became aware that this was a man rather than merely an automaton in a uniform. 'In asking you here, Mr Holmes, I have gone against centuries of tradition and will have almost certainly curtailed my own career. However, I am satisfied that neither I nor my staff possess the expertise to deal with this matter quickly and discreetly. I am therefore forced to place my trust in you.'

Holmes thought for several moments before responding in a quiet but authoritative tone. 'I will make every effort to bring this most unpleasant matter to a rapid conclusion, but I must be clear that I will require your total co-operation in every way and that you must implement my requests immediately and without question.'

The Rear-Admiral hesitated; for a man accustomed to giving orders, the very idea of total obedience to a civilian must have cut him to the quick. 'I am not sure I can accede to that, Mr Holmes. I am, after all, commander of this base and responsible for the men stationed here.'

'Then I must bid you good day, sir. I wish you every success in your prosecution of this matter. Come, Watson, we may still make the mid-afternoon train.' Holmes moved toward the ladder which we had descended only a little while before.

'Wait!' the Rear-Admiral commanded. 'You place me in a difficult position, Mr Holmes, but, as you are well aware, I have little alternative but to agree to your terms. I will ensure your every request is complied with.' The man's standing increased in my eyes as he spoke these words for, despite his every instinct, he was clearly also a pragmatic and rational leader.

'In that case, I will do all I can to resolve this affair, and I offer my word as a gentleman that I will endeavour to ensure that the reputation and fine tradition of the Navy is respected and upheld.'

The sincerity of Holmes' tone caused our host visibly to relax a little, although I became acutely aware of my own overwhelming desire to leave that place of death and regain the natural elements, no matter how harsh they might be.

*****

A quarter of an hour later, we were once again seated in the splendid office where we had first encountered the Rear-Admiral. A fire roared in the large grate. Holmes began to dictate his requirements in a measured tone. 'The HMS *Benbow* will put to sea tomorrow with exactly the same crew as before, but with the addition of Dr Watson and myself. We will remain at sea for forty-eight hours, during which time each man must conduct himself exactly as he did during the recent Mediterranean patrol. To be clear, each man will be stationed as before, will work, eat and sleep as before. In short, we must replicate exactly the conditions that prevailed on that fateful voyage.

'During our short excursion, we will not stop at any port and the captain must proceed as far from land as he can, given the time constraint. With my guidance, he will address the crew once we are well under way. Finally, the captain must be ordered to obey my every instruction without exception.'

The Rear-Admiral shook his head slowly. 'I can agree to all save one of your terms and will ensure that they are adhered to as if they were orders given by myself. But once a ship is at sea, the captain must have the final say on any matter that may jeopardise the safety and welfare of his vessel and her crew. The entire naval command structure is based upon this premise. If you will accept that the captain of HMS *Benbow* will submit to follow your every command, save only in the instance where doing so may endanger his ship, then we may proceed with preparations at once.'

Holmes steepled his fingers and turned his gaze toward the grand windows. For a brief moment it occurred to me that he was gazing into the future and weighing the implications of the Admiral's only proviso. 'Agreed,' said he.

*****

Holmes spent much of the rest of the day immersed in the Naval Library, while I retired to my room with some sandwiches and the daily papers. We dined in the officers' mess that evening, and both Holmes and I commented on the excellent quality of the food, though I think it fair to say that neither of us was particularly inclined toward eating. The horrible vision of the young man's lifeless face was never far from my mind, nor that of my companion, I was sure.

At eight o'clock sharp the following morning, I was rudely awoken by three forceful taps against my bedroom door. I had not slept especially well, finding that my mind had continually wandered back to the dreadful scene that had awaited Holmes and I deep in the bowels of the ship. Despite this, I was encouraged to see clear bright sunlight struggling to penetrate the heavy drapes of the sash window, even though my general mood was bleaker than I could remember.

I was starting to feel irritated by the effect the method of murder was having upon my spirits. Usually I would relish the opportunity of an adventure such as the one upon which we were about to embark but, try as I might, I could not shake myself free of a growing apprehension about what might lie in store.

At breakfast, Holmes was taciturn and reserved. When finally he spoke, I received little reassurance from his words and tone. 'This is a bad business, Watson. Very bad indeed. We must exercise vigilance and resolve as we have rarely had to. I am convinced that we will both keep our nerves steady to the end but we must ensure that, no matter the temptation or the circumstance, we never drop our guard even for an instant.'

I agreed wholeheartedly and was surprised to find myself taking a little comfort in the fact that my usually implacable colleague appeared also somewhat apprehensive as to what the day might bring. 'Holmes, I shall not fail. I will carry my sidearm at all times and will not hesitate to use it if events should so dictate.' I managed a small smile. 'Besides, it is a lovely day for a cruise.'

I was gratified that Holmes flashed a wry grin at my poor attempt at levity. 'Good old Watson. There is always a silver cloud somewhere, *n'est-ce pas?*'

*****

The *Benbow* looked magnificent as we strode toward her on the dockside. Steam poured from her funnels as the great pistons of her triple-expansion engines built up their momentum. She appeared almost to be straining at the leash, eager to leave shore and return once more to the oceans for which she was born. Great ropes, thicker than a man's arm, flexed taut and slack as her great bulk moved a few feet toward or away from the quayside.

I took out my hunter and noted that the time was a little before nine. In only ten minutes we would be leaving Portsmouth behind, venturing out into the Solent and from there past the Isle of Wight and into the Atlantic. Despite the ever-present feelings of foreboding, I felt my heart quicken and a thrill of excitement as we ventured up the gangplank. I paused at the top to take a deep breath of the cold clear air before ducking inside a doorway behind the receding back of Sherlock Holmes.

Minutes later Holmes and I found ourselves on the bridge being greeted by a man whose bearing, and the deference shown him by other men on station, clearly denoted that he was the captain of the vessel.

'I am Captain Charles Blandy and I welcome you aboard the HMS *Benbow*. I have received specific instructions from Rear-Admiral Caddington, and I understand what is required of me and my crew. I assure you that all my men will co-operate with your investigation most fully and to the best of their ability. May we first speak privately in my ready room?'

Blandy showed us into his private office adjacent to the main bridge. A pot of strong coffee was already on hand

and our host poured a cup for my colleague and me, which we accepted graciously.

'Thank you, Captain. The *Benbow* is a most impressive ship, and I am sure that her officers and crew are a credit to the service. Sadly, of course, there is certainly one aboard who is a most cruel and callous man. Until he is apprehended, none of us can be sure of the safety of this fine vessel and the men who sail in her.'

'Please be assured, Mr Holmes, that there is no one who shall be more pleased to see this sorry tale drawn to a rapid conclusion than I. But I must ask that you do nothing that may compromise the safety of the ship and her crew without consulting me first.' Behind the clear blue eyes, I could see flickers of anxiety and doubt.

'The Rear-Admiral and I have already discussed this matter and I'll give you the same answer as I gave him,' Holmes replied. 'I will do everything in my power to ensure that no lives, including those of Watson and myself, are put in jeopardy and that the *Benbow* is not placed at any unnecessary risk. However, you should be aware that we are undoubtedly dealing with a very dangerous man.'

Captain Blandy nodded that he understood.

*****

Holmes and I stood silently on the bridge as the order was given to get underway. Three great blasts on the ship's siren announced her impending departure, and slowly the mooring lines were cast off and she began to inch away from the quay. Almost imperceptibly at first, but then much more decisively, a growing rumble could be felt deep within the ship as the mighty engines began to increase their power, turning the massive twin screws that would propel us forward and out into the great expanse of the Atlantic.

The atmosphere on the bridge was one of quiet order and concentration. The helmsman stood erect, his unwavering gaze fixed upon the shipping lanes ahead. The captain sat in his chair, its base firmly fixed to the steel deck by heavy steel bolts. The first mate issued instructions to the wheelsman and presently, when we had left the land perhaps some thousand yards behind us, the captain gave the order to increase speed. The thrum of the engines increased. I could feel the vibration through the deck plate upon which I stood; it was as if the ship were truly coming alive and I marvelled at the ingenuity of man to create such a fabulous thing.

Holmes stepped out of the starboard bridge door and stood upon the flying deck. I followed him and revelled in the bracing breeze generated by our speed. The cold pale November sunlight danced upon the water, and the spray churned up by the *Benbow*'s razor bow looked like a stream of diamonds spreading out from the ship to become her wake.

Despite the seriousness of the deplorable business that had brought us here, I could not help grinning. 'Holmes! Isn't it wonderful?' I shouted over the roar of the wind and the surf.

My friend turned and flashed a quick smile, taking a deep breath of the salty air and exhaling slowly as if to savour its fortifying effects. Then he turned and nodded toward the bridge, a signal that it was time to get down to the business at hand.

*****

I spent an interesting but uneventful two hours wandering the ship while Holmes and Captain Blandy remained deep in conversation in the captain's ready room. I walked from stem to stern above deck, then slowly picked my way through the maze of bulkheads and compartments in the decks below in an attempt to orientate myself as fully as possible.

Everywhere there were men operating machinery, cleaning machinery, eating, sleeping, playing cards, reading, swabbing decks, steaming laundry; the list of tasks and occupations was endless. All were courteous but I could perceive curiosity and reserve behind their eyes. I would be treated as a guest, but I was clearly not one of them.

By the time I returned to the bridge, I felt I had assembled in my mind a reasonable map of the vessel that might enable me to aid Holmes' investigation. I found my friend waiting for me, a half-consumed pewter mug of tea in one hand, the other resting upon a brass railing to steady himself against the gentle rolling of the ship. We were now some thirty nautical miles or more from land and in deep waters.

'Ah, Watson, I trust you enjoyed your ramble. I need to commence a thorough reconnaissance of the ship. Will you join me?'

I indicated that I would be most happy to do so and that I felt sure I could act as guide. 'No need, Watson. I have glanced at the ship's plans and am now fully familiar with her layout. I think we shall start with the engine room – this way, I fancy.' And he started off at a brisk pace, taking the most direct route and never faltering as he led the way to the mighty beating heart of the ship.

*****

'Much as I expected,' shouted Holmes in my ear after we had observed the huge pistons endlessly cycling as the steam, under enormous pressure, drove the vast flywheel which in turn rotated the massive prop shaft that connected to the propeller and drove us forward. 'It is noisy enough here, and for several compartments around including the hold where Coggins met his end, that only someone very close by would hear cries of distress if they were issued.'

A few minutes later we had passed the marine on duty and were standing in the aforementioned hold. Although Holmes informed me that the remains of the hapless sailor had been removed, everything else remained just as we had seen it the day before. Even here, some distance from the engines, we had to raise our voices considerably and stand close together to converse with ease.

The great detective began one of his minute inspections lit by a powerful, portable, electric arc lamp in addition to the bulb that already burned in the ceiling mount. The effect was to render the compartment, which I could now judge was approximately fifteen feet by ten, almost unnaturally bright. It was much like an operating theatre, and I recalled with a shudder that such an analogy was not entirely inappropriate, given the events that had transpired there.

'The problem here is blood or the lack thereof, Watson,' said my friend after perhaps twenty minutes of careful scrutiny and detection. We had returned once again to the relative comfort of the main deck and the company of the most persistent gulls as they wheeled and cried before falling behind us.

I immediately nodded. 'I was thinking the same thing, Holmes. The brutal murder and dismemberment of a man would produce copious amounts of blood. Indeed, I would go so far as to suggest that at least five pints out of the total of nine would be lost from the body, and a considerable amount would be spilled upon the floor.'

'I entirely agree, Watson. Therefore, we must conclude that the murderer – or murderers, as I am beginning to believe – took great pains to clean the scene of the crime exceedingly thoroughly in order to minimise the residual evidence left behind. That implies that this atrocious destruction of a human life was not an irrational act, nor was it a crime born of passion or anger. The work is too clinical. I am forced to contemplate the possibility that it was a calculated murder considered necessary by the perpetrators for some reason known only to them at present.'

I listened attentively. Knowing how Holmes usually liked to keep his working theories carefully guarded until he was satisfied, I was slightly surprised that he was prepared to be so revealing at this stage.

As if he sensed my concerns, Holmes turned to me and said, 'This is a most dangerous business, my friend. Whoever perpetrated this crime is a cold-blooded killer who will not hesitate to kill again should they believe it essential to their aims. We must be on our constant guard here, Watson. Do not hesitate to draw my attention to any matter that you feel of note, no matter how trivial it may seem.'

I assured Holmes that I would not be reticent in making any observations known to him, and added a question of my own. 'Why do you think there may have been more than one murderer, Holmes?'

'That is a very significant question. Let us just say that at this stage I have no firm evidence to support such a hypothesis, but that my experience and intuition strongly suggest that this was the work of more than one man. The fact that they were able to clean the room so thoroughly indicates that they had a significant period of time after the deed that was uninterrupted. In order to achieve that, surely it is reasonable to assume that two men took it in turns, one keeping a watch while the other worked. If I am correct, then the implications for this case are profound.'

*****

At a little after half-past eleven Holmes and I stood on the fo'c'sle to the left of Captain Blandy, at whose instruction almost the entire ship's complement had been assembled on the main deck. The *Benbow* was near stationary but rolled gently with the swell. The men stood silently and at ease. First Officer Riggs stepped forward and at his word the crew snapped to attention.

Captain Blandy regarded his men silently for a moment then spoke clearly and audibly above the eternal sounds of the sea and the faint hum of the engines that had been reduced to an idle for his address.

'You are no doubt wondering why we have put to sea once again when we were all expecting well-earned shore leave. Despite your disappointment, you have all responded with the professionalism I would expect of this crew. It has been my pleasure and my honour to serve with you all these past six months, and I say without fear of challenge that this is the finest crew in the fleet.'

Both Holmes and I could plainly see the devotion and admiration in his men's eyes as the captain continued his address. 'But I must tell you of a most terrible crime that has befallen one of our own. All of you are aware that some weeks ago Able Seaman Coggins disappeared and was presumed lost overboard. I have to tell you now that he was in fact murdered in a most horrible and depraved manner.'

Despite their undoubted discipline, the assembled men were clearly grievously shocked by this terrible disclosure.

69

I saw some make the sign of the cross, while others appeared stunned as if by a hammer blow. I turned to Holmes to find him scrutinising the assembled mass with a piercing and unwavering gaze.

The captain paused for the crew to settle and then continued. 'The hard truth is that the murderer is one of our own. He most likely stands here before me, knowing what he has done and how he has betrayed us all.' Again Blandy paused for the full effect of his words to sink in.

'But he has made a serious miscalculation in his dreadful plans. For this man,' he turned and gestured towards my friend, 'is Mr Sherlock Holmes, the world-famous detective. And this,' he pointed to me, 'is Dr Watson, his valued assistant.'

I was acutely aware of more than a thousand eyes boring into me as each man settled his conscience and sized up my companion and me.

'They are here to find the murderer in our midst, the man who is not one of us. It is my instruction that you should render them your full co-operation and assistance as they might require it. You may assume Mr Holmes and Dr Watson act for me in this matter. That is all.'

As the men were dismissed and regained their duties above and below decks, Captain Blandy invited us to join him in his ready room adjacent to the bridge.

'Gentlemen, please be seated.' The captain was of a man of considerable presence and both Holmes and I followed his instruction, drawing up two simply carved but sturdy chairs.

'I will get straight to the point, Mr Holmes. As you are no doubt aware, upon your instruction I have just created an intolerable situation for my men. I have sown the seeds of disharmony and suspicion. For a while, maybe a day or so, the training and discipline of this crew will hold it together but beyond that I cannot say for sure. Each man will now be suspicious of his messmates, his section officers, his friends and his workmates. This is perhaps the most dangerous and damaging circumstance a crew can be placed in. Without trust, even the Royal Navy is little more than a collection of individuals, each with their own disparate needs. Without order and unity, we will not function effectively.'

Holmes listened quietly and attentively. 'You are correct, of course, and I recognise the overwhelming need for an expeditious conclusion to this sorry affair. I asked for two days at sea and now, as we sit here this noontime, I do not have any firm idea as to the identity of the killers.'

Captain Blandy's face gave little away but I could read in it the indications of great concern. Holmes undoubtedly noticed these also, as there were few men more adept at reading others than he.

'However, I am not entirely without avenues of inquiry,' Holmes said, 'and I remain convinced that a resolution to this case may be possible during the next thirty-six hours.'

Our host smiled thinly. 'I pray that you are correct, Mr Holmes, I surely do.'

Holmes turned to me. 'Come, it is time for us to visit the purser. I wish to know more about the ill-fated Coggins.'

*****

Several ladders and passageways later, Holmes and I arrived outside the heavy bulkhead door that bore a small brass plaque stating that it was indeed the Purser's Office. The door was slightly ajar; Holmes pushed it wide with a firm shove and nimbly stepped over the six-inch-high lip that formed the base of all doors below deck and most above it.

Inside we found the purser sitting at his desk, diligently entering numbers into a large ledger. The small office was lit by two portholes and an electric reading light was positioned over the desk. The purser looked up, and I saw him to be a man some years older than the majority of the crew. I was not surprised by this as I knew that the job required an experience with figures and management that often required a degree of maturity and knowledge beyond many younger men.

The role of purser is one of those most essential yet holds little glamour or attraction for most. When one thinks of 'going to sea' with the Royal Navy, one usually thinks of hardened sailors battling the elements or dashing officers commanding massive firepower in a battle to smash the enemy to smithereens. I think it is fair to say that one rarely gives consideration to the financial and logistical management required to maintain a large body of men, perhaps many hundreds in number, in good health and spirits halfway across the world.

A purser needed to be able to negotiate with locals from other cultures for provisions, to manage the ship's consumable resources in conjunction with the quartermaster and other ranks, to ensure men were paid appropriately, and to assist the captain with many aspects of the smooth running of a ship many thousands of miles from its home port. It was a skilled role that usually went to a man who had served in a number of positions for some years. It was also a position only given to men who had shown themselves to be of excellent and trustworthy character.

At the same time the purser looked up, I noted that another smaller desk tucked away against the far wall was vacant. It was obvious that this had been the workplace of his ill-fated assistant.

Holmes strode forward and shook hands warmly with the large man who had risen to greet us. 'Mr Goodhall, I presume? I am so sorry to arrive unannounced, but I take it you expected that we would be dropping by soon?'

'Indeed I did, sir, and I will be most happy to assist you in any way that I can, although I will state now that I don't think I will have much to contribute to your investigation.'

'Well, let us see. Perhaps you will be able to confirm a few small matters that have been troubling me. For instance, were you aware of any men with whom young Coggins had differences?'

'Oh no, sir, definitely not,' replied the purser emphatically. 'I have met few men more popular than young Arthur was. He was one of those people you can't help but warm to. He was friendly and always polite, and I am certain he was very well-liked throughout the crew.'

'I see. That is most helpful. Tell me, were you happy with his work?'

'His work was generally of a high standard. Whenever he made an error, he would immediately bring it to my attention and do his best to rectify the situation. He was,' the purser suddenly appeared moved, 'a thoroughly decent young man whom I held in the highest esteem.'

'And in the days before his disappearance did Arthur appear distracted or ill at ease in any way?'

'No sir, not as far as I could tell. He spoke of his young lady who was waiting for him back home; he even showed me a picture. Nice looking lass. She must be very upset.'

'No doubt,' said Holmes sadly. 'As always in these matters, it is the families and their loved ones who often suffer the most.'

On many occasions, I have commented upon Holmes' remarkable ability to control conversations and to empathise and communicate with his subjects in just the right way so as to elicit information that would have otherwise gone unremarked and unnoticed. Holmes now played a masterstroke. 'Did young Arthur have any peculiarities of habit or customs that you can recollect?'

The purser thought for a moment. 'Well now, I wouldn't say it was a peculiarity, but for a young man he was not a heavy sleeper. Quite often he would roam the ship during his time off-watch. He always said he liked the exercise and the company. I believe it is because he was so often about the ship that he made so many friends and was so well known and well regarded.'

I glanced at Holmes and observed a familiar gleam in his eye. It was obvious that he regarded the purser's information as highly significant. The detective continued his questioning for a few minutes more before thanking Goodhall for his help and ushering me back out to the corridor.

Holmes then took out his pocket watch and remarked, 'Right on time,' before hurrying off toward the stern. Presently we arrived at the officers' mess. Upon entering, we found a man dressed in apron and chef's hat standing to attention beside the heavy oak table that formed the centrepiece of the room.

'Yes, yes, at ease,' said Holmes with a smile. 'Please sit down. Seaman Oxley, isn't it?'

The cook appeared uneasy. 'Sir, I haven't been able to speak to any of my shipmates since I came back aboard. Tell me, am I under suspicion? 'Cos if I am, I swear, sir, I 'ad nothing to do with young Coggins' end. I liked the lad, we all did. 'E was a regular character with not a bad bone in 'is body.'

Holmes held up a hand. 'Please be assured, Oxley, that at present I do not have any particular suspicions in your direction, although I am beginning to perceive some features of significance elsewhere. I merely wish to discuss the circumstances of the sad discovery of Arthur Coggin's body.'

The cook nodded and appeared to relax a little. 'I will do my best to 'elp any which way I can, sir, you can be sure of that.'

Holmes nodded. 'Please relate the events of that morning as clearly as you can. I would be grateful if you could keep speculation to a minimum for the moment.'

As it transpired, the cook was a surprisingly good witness in that he was careful to relate the facts in chronological order and avoided embellishment or fancy.

'It was about a quarter to eight in the morning. Store Room Six, that was where I was headin''. It holds mainly long storage stuff – y'know, the kind of food and drink that lasts a good few months at least. I needed some cooking oil, which was held in one of the wall casks. I drained some off using the little tap but the colour looked very dark, certainly not as it should, so I opened up the top. It was then that I saw the…'

The cook hesitated, clearly repulsed by the memory. 'That was when I saw 'is arm, sir. I'm ashamed to tell you, I hollered out loud and ran outside to get the first officer I could. It just so 'appened it was Master Riggs with several other men. He immediately took charge and sent for the captain. I remained inside the storeroom while the captain and his first officer looked about, then the Cap told me to report to 'is ready room and not to tell a soul 'bout what I had seen.

'Well, an order is an order and I was determined to do exactly as I was told. I 'urried along to the Cap'n and then spent the remaining two days before we got 'ome in his quarters on my own. The Cap was very decent about it and made sure I wanted for nothing. Don't mind telling you, I quite enjoyed me time and spent most of it readin' one of your excellent books.'

The cook nodded toward Holmes and I found myself smiling in return, although my friend seemed entirely unmoved. 'That is as may be, but please do not give too much credence to any of those little flights of fancy, my good man. They may be entertaining in their own way, but there is little of factual merit within them.'

I almost bridled at Holmes' rudeness but quickly stopped myself when I noticed a sly glance from my friend. As readers of some of my other accounts have probably noted, Holmes sometimes displays a streak of devilment with regards to my humble scribblings and has taken the opportunity to prick my pride on more than one occasion.

I sighed with the exaggerated resignation of a man who must bear more than his fair share of trials, and expressed my hope that the cook had enjoyed it.

Holmes questioned the cook at considerable length and in great detail before pronouncing himself satisfied and dismissing the helpful sailor. 'This is a difficult case, Watson, and I am certain that there are great depths to it that so far elude me. I am going to take my leave of you now and go forth among the crew to make some enquiries. I shall be a couple of hours or so, and then we shall have a late lunch in the officers' mess. In the meantime, I would counsel you not to drop your guard for an instant.'

It was not until nearly three o'clock that I saw Holmes again. The weather had taken a decided turn for the worse and my stroll around deck had been curtailed by the return of the rain from the day before. Within a short space of time a heavy sleet had begun, and the clear sky had vanished to be replaced by ominous clouds that seemed to merge with the grey sea. Holmes returned deep in thought, and it was only after I had declared myself famished that he consented to partake of some victuals in the officers' mess.

I ate a hearty lunch of gammon, fried potatoes and eggs with strong tea and freshly baked rye bread while Holmes, as was his custom when engaged in serious thought, sat silently and occasionally picked at his repast. It was only after more than half an hour and half a dozen cigarettes that he spoke.

'I have talked to a great many crew who might be considered to have been working in close proximity to young Coggins, and none have been able to shed any significant light upon his demise. Indeed, the most remarkable and significant feature of my morning's investigations is how little I have learned that is of value.

'I am therefore forced to consider that the murderer or murderers are skilled men with considerable experience at remaining hidden and giving nothing away. Further, it is becoming clear that in order to make progress and expose them, I may need to take singular and unusual measures.'

'You mean to smoke them out?' I asked using a term we had seized upon in Afghanistan.

Holmes looked at me thoughtfully. 'Yes, I believe that is the essence of what I am proposing. I must force them to show their hands.'

Regular readers will recall that Holmes has used such tactics on more than one occasion. For example, he created a false conflagration in the home of Irene Adler to compel her to reveal the location of a sought-after photograph. He had also used a similar tactic in the peculiar case of The Norwood Builder, with spectacular results.

'I am convinced that we are dealing with very clever men who have killed because they wished to hide something, or to silence young Coggins because he had somehow, perhaps inadvertently, stumbled across information dangerous to their position.'

Although I knew Holmes often relied upon not only his vast experience and knowledge of crime but also upon his finely tuned instincts, I was still surprised at the amount of supposition he appeared to be making, and I told him so.

'You are right, of course, my dear Watson. But perhaps you will indulge me while I explain. This is one of those instances when I would very much welcome your opinion, as you are the oxygen that may fire my imagination.'

Holmes had once before claimed that, while I was not luminescent in myself, I had the rare ability to reflect and magnify his own brilliance. I was delighted that my friend not only needed me but also was placing so much value upon my opinion.

'Of course, Holmes. I will do my very best to consider the facts and theories you place before me and make any pertinent observations that I can.'

'Well then, let us consider the bare facts for a moment. Firstly, we have a most abominable and gruesome murder that has been perpetrated upon an apparently very well-thought-of young man. As far as I can tell, he was universally liked and had no enemies. The murderers,' I noted that Holmes was now using the plural, 'not only had the presence of mind to slay young Coggins in cold blood but also to see through the most unpleasant task of dismembering his body and concealing its parts.'

'Why did they simply not throw the body overboard?' I asked. The question seemed obvious and indeed Holmes had a convincing answer.

'I have pondered that very question, and the conclusion must be that to carry a body from the lower decks to the sea deck would have been too risky. I have made the journey several times and on no occasion did I encounter less than twenty other crew members. No, our murderers had no choice but to attempt to hide the body in such a way as to stand a good chance that discovery would not occur until they had returned to port, at which point they may well have had the opportunity to quietly remove the traces of their crime.

'Secondly, they must have had a very good reason to perpetrate such an act. I believe that it was a murder without pre-planning, otherwise there would have been easier ways to dispose of Coggins – perhaps by throwing him overboard, as you mentioned. Also, I believe that Coggins was the kind of young man that, if he had discovered something underhand or stumbled across some dastardly scheme amongst several members of the crew, would have reported it immediately. All the men I have spoken to have all insisted he was a thoroughly honest member of the crew.'

I nodded vigorously. It was always a privilege to witness the working of Holmes' incredible intellect. As he verbalised his thoughts, I was struck by how subtle and plausible was his reasoning.

'Therefore I must consider the possibility that Coggins, perhaps while on one of his late-night sojourns around the ship, stumbled across two or more men engaged in an activity so serious that, had he revealed its nature, there would have been the most disastrous repercussions for those responsible. Therefore, these miscreants acted without hesitation or compassion and slew him. They bear all the hallmarks of professional men and therefore are likely to be more difficult to apprehend.'

I agreed that this seemed a reasonable explanation. 'So what in heaven's name could it be that Coggins found?'

'At present I have no idea, although I am sure of one thing: it must have been near to where he was murdered as he had no time to escape or raise an alarm. However, given that we have no clue as to what we are looking for, I think we need to encourage the guilty to aid us in our investigation.'

Holmes excused himself and left me to an excellent almond pudding, saying that he needed to discuss matters with Captain Blandy. 'In the meantime, I would be grateful if you could spend some time inspecting the compartments immediately adjacent to the scene of the crime. Please be thorough and note any features that may be of interest or appear unusual. Make sure you also speak to any men that may pass and see if you can elicit any further information. Be careful to tell them that you are searching the area thoroughly. I will join you shortly.'

*****

It was more than an hour later that Holmes joined me and I expressed my regret that I had little to report, despite having spoken to at least a dozen curious sailors who had passed by. Holmes, far from appearing disappointed, was apparently impressed. 'Excellent work, Watson. I am sure your efforts will illicit results before the night is passed. Now we must secure this murder room sufficiently to appear that we are serious, but not so securely as to prevent a determined man from gaining access.

'Further, we shall remain here overnight ready to apprehend our suspects when they show their faces. Captain Blandy and his first officer will conceal themselves in suitable hiding places within a few yards of us, ready to leap to our assistance when we give the signal. You will appreciate that it is only the captain and his first officer whom I have been able to take into any degree of confidence, for I have not been able to rule out the involvement of other senior members of the crew.

'Finally, Watson, I beg of you to remain steadfast and alert. There is no doubt that we face a dangerous and deadly foe who has already killed and will not hesitate to do so again should they be cornered or their dastardly schemes exposed.'

Holmes reached inside his coat and removed a Webley revolver of the latest type. He handed it to me without comment but his eyes conveyed his intent most clearly. 'I am also armed. Although I would like to apprehend these men alive, should that not prove possible I will not hesitate to shoot.'

I nodded. I admit I was beginning to feel most apprehensive in a way I had rarely felt before. Perhaps it was Holmes' gravitas; perhaps it was the fact that he was carrying a gun, an event he did not make a habit of, or perchance it was simply a degree of intuition. Regardless, as I have said previously, I was not a man prone to a nervous disposition and I resolved silently that I would remain resolute in the face of any dangers we might be required to face.

'But Holmes, how can you be sure the killer will show his face tonight?' Although Holmes appeared confident, I could not perceive from whence this confidence might originate.

'I cannot be entirely sure but, on the balance of probability, I think it highly likely. I have no doubt that your efforts have not gone unnoticed and that the ship's rumour mill will work in our favour. The killers will by now be aware that we are searching for something they will be most desirous to keep from us. Whatever it is, they may fear that we are very close to finding it. Further, they will also be aware that we are only at sea for forty-eight hours and therefore time is a commodity in which they are in short supply.'

'Holmes, do you have any idea as to the motivation behind this murder?' To my mind, this was the key to the whole case.

Holmes confirmed he was thinking along the same lines. 'I do have some ideas but I cannot yet be sure. Be under no illusion though, Watson. If I am right, the repercussions may shake the Empire to its very core.'

Although I pressed, Holmes would say no more and the two of us retired to positions within the quartermaster's stores. I crouched behind some barrels and Holmes screened himself behind a tarpaulin.

I was ready for a long night of waiting but it transpired that the events of that evening were to take an unexpected and deadly turn that would threaten not only our own lives but also those of the entire crew – and the very existence of the *Benbow* herself.

*****

It was difficult to be certain but perhaps four hours had passed. In the total darkness of the storeroom that Holmes and I inhabited, it was only my expectation and excitement that prevented me from falling asleep. Even so, it was hard not to let my mind wander; I found myself conjuring up all kinds of explanations, each less credible than the last, for the strange and disturbing murder of an apparently popular and well-regarded young man.

It was just as I was discounting yet another implausible theory that Holmes called out softly. Moments later, I heard the sounds of the heavy wheel lock on the storeroom door being turned carefully and tentatively. In the faint light of the corridor, I saw a man silhouetted for a moment before he stepped quietly through the entrance and turned to close the door behind him.

There followed an agony of seconds where Holmes and I dared not breathe as our guest satisfied himself he was alone and no one was about to enter the compartment behind him. A match was struck and a small lantern, its wick three-quarters screened, cast a very narrow dim beam around the room. Again the man waited.

Then, as if he had had enough and was desirous to get his business over with as quickly as possible, the dark figure moved quickly across the floor to the heavy piping that criss-crossed the interior of the hull. I listened as there were some faint scratching sounds and a series of clicks.

'Get him, Watson!' Holmes yelled, as he launched himself across the space that divided him from his quarry. I immediately leapt to his aid and recall in the confusion seeing the startled face of a swarthy-looking man who immediately reached toward a pipe and appeared to fumble inside.

I grabbed at the man and the lantern fell to the floor but fortunately maintained its flame. In the half-light, I recall seeing Holmes bring his gun up to the man's face and then he said, 'It is over. Be still or I will shoot.'

Our subject froze. 'Alright, you have me,' he growled. 'I'll not resist further.'

Holmes quickly strode to the door and flung it open, his attention never wavering from the man whose arms I now had pinned behind him. Holmes gave three short, shrill blasts on a whistle he retrieved from his pocket and within moments we were joined by Captain Blandy and First Officer Riggs, both carrying bright gas lamps.

'Why, it's Bradstreet! He's one of the ship's carpenters and handymen,' exclaimed Riggs when he cast his eyes upon our prisoner.

The man stared back insolently but said nothing.

'Mr Holmes, you have caught the murderer! Congratulations are in order, and I'll look forward to seeing this man swing for what he has done.'

'I only wish that this were the end to the case but I am far from sure that it is,' said Holmes. 'Please bring the light over here.'

He moved to the hull where Bradstreet had been engaged. One of the pipes appeared to have had an end cap removed. Holmes took the lamp and peered inside. Even by the harsh glare of the lantern, I am sure that I saw his face turn white.

Captain Blandy caught his look and also examined the inside of the pipe. 'Great heavens! What on earth is that?'

Holmes' voice was eerily calm as he said, 'It is a bomb, sir, with a timer fuse. And it is set to detonate less than six hours from now.'

For a moment no one spoke.

*****

Within minutes a sentry had been posted to secure the compartment. Our party, with Bradstreet at gunpoint, had

86

proceeded to the captain's ready room. Here our prisoner was seated in a chair, his arms and legs bound tightly before Holmes finally lowered his pistol.

'You realise you face the rope?' my friend enquired in a chilling voice. Our charge's only reply was silence. 'We have discovered the bomb and we shall defuse it shortly.'

Our captive looked at each of us; his unwavering gaze was most unsettling, and I found myself almost recoiling as he stared at me and smiled. I shall never forget the look of assured superiority with which he favoured me at that moment. Indeed, I remember the instant that our eyes locked as one of the pivotal of my life, for suddenly I understood what was happening,

'Holmes!' I began to speak.

My friend held up his hand. 'You are right, Watson. There is more than one bomb, as there is also more than one murderer.'

I saw the colour drain from Captain Blandy's face as the horrible realisation that his ship and almost certainly her crew were doomed. He advanced on Bradstreet and struck the man across his face. 'You will tell us where to find them and who your accomplice is.'

Our prisoner, blood trickling at the corner of his mouth, sneered. His contempt was clear. 'I will tell you nothing, you swine,' he spat.

Holmes took charge. 'Captain, how far are we from port?'

'At least eight hours at full steam. We will never make it back in time.'

Holmes thought for a moment, then said, 'And how far are we from any land, Captain?'

'Perhaps six hours. I will have to consult the charts.'

'Then you must set a course for the nearest beach or sandbank and steam at maximum speed until you run aground.' With growing horror, I realised that Holmes was describing the only viable chance of survival and saving the ship.

Captain Blandy hesitated, but only for an instant. 'You are right, Mr Holmes. It is our only option.' He turned to his first officer and confirmed his order with a nod. Moments later, the thrum of the mighty engines started to build and the *Benbow* turned hard to port as it sought to reverse its course and regain the land once more.

*****

The ship's clocks indicated that the time was a quarter past midnight. The *Benbow*, operating on a three-shift system, was at night watch. Theoretically, two-thirds of the complement were asleep although the noise of the engines had undoubtedly roused some who now sat huddled in their messes, smoking and speculating as to the cause of the diversion.

When engaged upon a case, Holmes seemed to require no sleep whatsoever. He had ventured out onto deck clutching a large mug of strong tea, an oilskin drawn tightly around him to protect him from the strong gusts and rapidly worsening weather. The *Benbow* flung herself at the waves, her engines almost flying apart as they fought to maintain her incredible speed of more than twenty knots.

Holmes had revisited the bomb and declared that it was a fine piece of engineering, but he would be unable to render it safe. He had then taken Captain Blandy and me to one side and explained the full scale of his fears.

'Gentlemen, Bradstreet has an accomplice, of that I have no doubt. He will never knowingly betray him. Further, I am convinced that there is more than one bomb on board this ship and that by now the others will have been primed. We have little chance of finding them and, even if we do, no hope of defusing them.' Holmes spoke evenly, his voice betraying no emotion.

'Our only hope of saving the ship and communicating what has happened to the Admiralty, is to make land before the explosives detonate. I am of the belief that we have stumbled upon a much larger conspiracy here which, if I am correct, threatens our nation as few things have before.'

I pressed him, but Holmes was not yet prepared to reveal his conclusions. I also took the opportunity to point out another unsavoury course of action that was open to us. 'Holmes, if it looks like we have no hope, you must take to a lifeboat and perhaps be saved. What you have learned cannot be allowed to die with you.'

My friend looked at me and declared that he had considered such a possibility. 'But we are not beaten yet, Watson! I am working on several ideas.' He turned and continued staring out into the night.

*****

I was awoken by Holmes urgently shaking me. I sat up and mumbled my apology, ashamed that I had fallen asleep after lying down for a few minutes in my cabin.

'Come, Watson, we are back in the game. I need you to visit our prisoner and administer a little rum under the auspices of checking his circulation and general health.'

As we hurried toward the bridge, Holmes outlined what I can only describe in retrospect as one of his most audacious plans. I confess I was not confident of its success but, as my friend pointed out, there was little to lose.

I entered the brig, where Bradstreet had been confined during the night. His hands and feet were still tied. I told him I was a doctor and wished to check his circulation then loosened the bonds, professing myself a little concerned. Befriending the man, I offered him a healthy tot of rum which was received stonily; it was clear he was not keen to engage in conversation. However, with a conspiratorial smile I offered him another large slug of rum, which he tossed back with only a moment's hesitation.

I refastened his bonds, ensured they were not too tight then retreated. Holmes, the captain and a crewman were waiting for me. Holmes introduced me to the sailor, whose name he said was Brown, and explained that we should wait a little while 'for Dr Watson's expertly administered medicine to lower our captive's guard a little'.

After perhaps five minutes, Holmes bade our new companion push the door ajar and kneel at its entrance. Holmes, Captain Blandy and I retreated around a corner in the corridor. I listened intently and made out a ferocious, whispered conversation between Brown and Bradstreet. Although I could hear the sounds, I was unable to make out any words no matter how hard I listened. It was as if they were speaking another language which, all of a sudden, I realised was exactly the case. Presently the conversation ceased and Brown pushed the door closed.

Holmes led us back quickly toward the bridge and Captain Blandy's ready room. 'Brown is actually *Braun*, my dear Watson. Captain Blandy has used him on numerous occasions as an interpreter,' he said as soon as we were all seated, with Captain Blandy perched on the edge of his desk.

'I kept turning over the few words that Bradstreet uttered upon being apprehended and I realised that there was one word that didn't sound right. He called our good captain here a 'swine' but, as I replayed the insult in my mind, I became ever more convinced that there had been an inflection. As you know, Watson, I have a very finely tuned ear for accents. Although it would be virtually imperceptible to anyone else, I was sure I had identified a native German speaker. The word 'swine' and '*schwein*' have exactly the same meaning in both languages, and both can be used as an insult. However, no matter how good Bradstreet's spoken English, in that moment of anguish his mask slipped. Now he has proved it beyond any doubt by conversing fully with Brown in German, believing him to be his confederate. It is a point of note that it is surprisingly difficult to recognise a voice when it is whispered.'

I was astonished. 'So you had me administer alcohol to loosen his tongue a little. And then Brown here,' I nodded at the sailor, 'masqueraded as his accomplice! My God, Holmes, it is fantastic even by your standards!'

'Not really, Watson. It was, as they say, a shot to nothing. I had little to lose by playing the only card I had. Depending on what Brown has to tell us, it may now prove an ace or a deuce.'

Over the next fifteen minutes Holmes expertly debriefed the steadfast sailor who, it appeared, had played his part admirably well.

*****

At half-past two o'clock, Holmes roused me from my nap by roughly shaking me awake. My companion had insisted that I attempt to get some rest, stating that we would need to be fully alert if we were to see this matter through to a positive conclusion. I am not a man who has much difficulty in enjoying my bed; indeed, Holmes had remarked on more than one occasion about my ability to fall fast asleep even in the most fraught circumstances.

Blinking away the remnants of an hour's rest, I observed his earnest expression. 'Watson, we must ready ourselves for the coming trials. The very survival of the *Benbow* may depend upon us and our ability to act at the decisive moment.

'If my analysis is correct, we have perhaps two hours to prepare for the conclusion of this case. I have already discussed my theories with Captain Blandy and he concurs with my hypothesis.' Holmes went on to explain in detail exactly what he expected to transpire and the role I was expected to play in the dénouement.

I listened very carefully. 'It is without doubt very risky, Holmes, but I agree that we appear to have few alternatives. I will do my utmost to carry out your instructions.'

'Excellent!' Holmes grasped my shoulder. 'If we live through this, we will undoubtedly have rendered a most valuable service to our Queen and country.'

I heartily agreed but felt compelled to point out that if we were *un*successful, the repercussions could hardly be more disastrous.

*****

Less than half an hour later, Holmes and I stood on the bridge staring out to sea as the *Benbow* continued to thrust herself forward with immense power, the engines shaking the mighty ship from bow to stern. Captain Blandy sat in his chair, his eyes constantly scanning the horizon then flicking ceaselessly around the bridge, across the binnacle, over the banks of gauges and dials and back out toward the as-yet invisible coastline.

Despite the noise and the energy that pulsed through the ship and the constant pitching and rolling, the bridge was a scene of calm and concentration. At the map table

First Officer Commander Riggs pored over his charts, determining our exact location and issuing orders for corrections to our course. Second Officer Lieutenant Locke, a dark-haired man with broad shoulders, stood at the windows with heavy naval glasses raised to his eyes.

All of the senior crew glanced repeatedly at the large brass-cased clock mounted above the centre of the substantial glass windows that afforded us a panoramic view of the boiling sea.

The *Benbow* flung herself against the awesome forces of nature with a furious might that seemed to cleave the sea in two. Every few moments the bows disappeared as the ship charged through yet another colossal wave, only to re-emerge with thousands of gallons of freezing water streaming from her deck. Without doubt it was an incredible sight, and the urgency of our flight added to the intense drama of the battle between machine and Poseidon's fury.

'Twenty-one knots, sir, and holding steady.' The helmsman called out our astonishing speed at regular intervals.

Captain Blandy turned to us and shouted over the terrific din, 'I doubt if any ship has ever gone faster in such weather!' Even given the desperate circumstances, there was no mistaking the pride in his voice.

I thought about what it must be like down in the engine room where the immense high-pressure steam engines, the very latest in naval technology, must have been on the verge of shaking free of their mountings while the boilers burned hotter than the fires of hell itself.

I lost track of time in these extraordinary circumstances, but I was acutely aware of the constant lurching of the deck beneath my feet, and I recall being extremely grateful that I had never suffered from sea-sickness. Holmes continued to scan the bridge and the five officers and men who were upon it.

'Ten miles to landfall,' the second officer, who had taken over the charts, called out.

Captain Blandy acknowledged his words with a grim smile. 'She will either make it or we will perish in the deep water off South Bank almost within sight of Pompey.'

'We have less than half an hour. It is going to be a very close call.' Holmes appeared to be coiled for action; indeed, both the captain and I were very conscious that, if my friend was correct in his reasoning, events were about to take a most decisive turn.

I looked at Holmes and he silently asked if I was ready. I nodded almost imperceptibly in return.

Suddenly the *Benbow* seemed to become airborne as she strove to bridge the trough between two mighty whitecaps. There followed what felt like an eternity of falling before a colossal crash and shockwave as her keel smashed into the heaving black Atlantic. To my right there was a loud report; in the confusion, I saw the helmsman slump to the deck.

Within moments, the second officer was at the wheel, wrestling with it as if it were alive. I became aware that he was struggling to turn it hard to starboard. The *Benbow* shuddered and lurched as her bows came around at maximum speed.

For a second my mind refused to make sense of what I was seeing, then the awful realisation struck. Second Officer Locke had shot the helmsman and was turning the *Benbow* away from the shore and back toward deep water. Just as Holmes had predicted to Captain Blandy and I several hours previously, Bradstreet's accomplice could not permit us to make land. Indeed, so great were the stakes that he would choose to perish rather than allow his secret to be exposed.

Holmes advanced on Locke, but the second officer trained his firearm on my friend and fired without hesitation. In that instant I froze, but the ship had lurched disrupting his aim and Captain Blandy seized the moment to launch himself at the treacherous officer. He managed to grasp Locke in a bear hug as another shot, this time muffled, rang out.

I saw Captain Blandy's hold on his man begin to slip. As he fell to the deck, both Holmes and I retrieved our revolvers from our holsters. Moving as one, we took aim at the treasonous lieutenant and fired simultaneously, hitting him at virtually point-blank range. Locke died instantly, hit in both the head and the heart by two heavy calibre slugs.

I immediately knelt and checked Blandy for his vital signs. The courageous captain was still conscious but it took only a glance to realise that the wound was mortal. Holmes and Riggs immediately corrected our course, and suddenly one of the watch officers cried out the words all sailors long to hear: 'Land ahoy!'

I felt the great ship swinging around as she sought to regain her original course and then Holmes shouted, 'Less than two minutes!' Even in the confusion, I knew he was referring to the remaining time before the explosives would detonate, sending the noble ship and all those aboard her to the bottom of the angry channel.

And then came a mighty shuddering and a deafening shrieking of tortured metal as the *Benbow* began to run aground on the sand of South Bank. The huge momentum of the massive 10,000-ton ship continued to drive her forward, ramming her into the beach, while on the bridge charts and people were thrown through the air as the *Benbow* ground to a halt.

As everything stopped moving, there came a succession of muffled roars from deep within the ship. The *Benbow* shuddered three final times as the explosives ripped through her hull; just as her captain and second officer had been struck by mortal blows, so the ship herself shook as she bore her wounds.

I looked down at the face of Captain Blandy, whose head I was cradling in my arms. As the great ship came to a full rest he smiled. 'Well done, Mr Holmes,' he said weakly before he passed away.

*****

It was more than twenty-four hours before Holmes and I were sitting once more in Rear-Admiral Caddington's office. The rescue of the *Benbow*'s crew had been forced to remain in abeyance until the weather had abated, but fortunately Commander Riggs had risen to the occasion and ensured her crew were kept safe and informed. Indeed, Holmes and I had received several moving votes of thanks for our efforts, although the tragic loss of Captain Blandy was source of great pain for all.

Despite our confinement to the ship, Holmes had ensured that a sealed tube containing a brief note was transferred from the *Benbow* and sent ahead of us to the Admiralty at Portsmouth.

My friend and I now sat in large easy chairs opposite a board comprised of some of the most senior figures in Her Majesty's Royal Navy. The debriefing that followed was to take some three hours, during which time two clerks made careful and independent notes.

After introductions had been made, Rear-Admiral Caddington bade Holmes tell the complete story sparing no detail. Holmes, whose mind recorded events with unerring accuracy and clarity, spoke almost continuously for two hours, pausing only to answer a few questions on minor points and technicalities.

'Gentlemen, I will not pretend that this was in any way an ordinary case. It so transpired that the stakes were almost without parallel in my career and indeed, I suspect, the history of the Royal Navy.

'When Rear-Admiral Caddington first took us aboard the *Benbow* and revealed to us the horrible nature of the murder that had occurred, I felt immediately that this was a crime with great depths. My instincts, honed after years of experience, cried out that here was a case whose implications would be profound. At that stage, I had no hard evidence for my opinions, but as the case developed all the facts seemed to correspond with my beliefs. I will admit that I also considered other possibilities, including an unsavoury crime of passion, but all the circumstances of the death suggested cold calculation and the involvement of more than one perpetrator.

'Fortunately, Rear-Admiral Caddington had taken excellent and decisive steps to ensure the quarantine of the crew and preserve the integrity of the crime scene. These steps, in particular the isolation of the crew, allowed me to formulate a risky but decisive plan.

'I realised that here was an opportunity to resolve this case before the heat of the act had fully dissipated – to strike while the iron was still hot, if you will. I was sure that if we could take immediate and positive steps we might be able to solve the crime with dispatch.

'I therefore requested that we put to sea immediately and re-create the conditions under which the murder had taken place. My intention was to force the murderers to reveal themselves by making them believe I was about to reveal them and their purpose.

'I was quickly able to satisfy myself that the poor departed Able Seaman Coggins was unlikely to be part of a deadly plot, unless unwittingly. As it turned out, that was indeed the case. Many witnesses attested to his character and integrity, but also they told me of his habit of late-night rambling around the ship. This was a critical clue; it offered the possibility that Coggins might have stumbled across something that left his murderers with no choice but to kill him immediately and without mercy. It suggested a much bigger plot that involved more than one man and required them to take absolutely no chance of it being revealed before their schemes could reach fruition.

'Given that I was becoming convinced of a professional element to this murder, I then had to speculate as to the types of person that could have perpetrated it, together with their motivation. Captain Blandy and I spoke at some length on this matter, and he revealed to me that there were currently concerns about increased activity from a number of potential enemies of the Crown.

'With the help of Watson and the ship's unofficial telegraph system, I was able to put the word about that we were close to making discoveries crucial to the resolution of the matter. This forced the hand of the wrongdoers and we closed the trap swiftly and resolutely on the man calling himself Bradstreet.

'It was with the apprehension of this culprit that my fears were confirmed. There could be no dispute that he was a professional man and not merely a ship's carpenter. I satisfied myself we had the actual murderer when I checked the workshop and found a saw that had been boiled clean. There is no doubt in my mind that this was the instrument used for the dismemberment of the unfortunate Coggins. However, the discovery of an explosive device carefully placed and primed to sink the ship could be nothing other than the act of agents of a foreign power. According to the discussion I had had with Captain Blandy, there were at least three foreign powers that could have been behind this most ingenious and deadly plot.

'It was then that I had a little luck: for the briefest of moments, this man let his impeccable, salt-of-the-earth British accent slip. Probably only someone such as I, who has made a study of such things and has subsequently developed a finely tuned ear, would have detected it. I was sure that he was German, and therefore acting for the new Kaiser.

'I formulated a simple but bold plan to trick him into revealing more than he wished. While any of us can recognise a voice, none of us can do the same to any degree of accuracy with a whisper. Therefore, with Watson here ensuring the man had imbibed enough rum to impair his judgement slightly, I coached Braun, whose mother was German and who himself spoke the language fluently, to pretend to be Bradstreet's accomplice. I knew I could trust him as Captain Blandy had assured me that Braun had never hidden his heredity and was proud of his German antecedents.

'The conversation confirmed that there was indeed a terrible plot of such import that these dedicated men were prepared to pay with their lives to ensure it was not uncovered.

'On my word, Captain Blandy had set course for the nearest land with the hope that we might reach it before the remaining charges exploded and sent the *Benbow* to the bottom of the Atlantic with the dreadful secret we now held. I was convinced that the unknown accomplice was highly placed within the senior staff; only someone on the bridge could hope to take decisive action to prevent our reaching land.

'I was also sure that the agent would remain hidden until the last moment. He would only reveal himself when he believed there was a significant chance that we would be saved and there was so little time left that he could hold the wheel by force of arms.

'I was correct in my reasoning. Although I had not suspected Locke, I was not entirely surprised to find out it was he. I only regret that a man as fine as Captain Blandy had to die to secure the salvation of the *Benbow*, although I know the as captain would not have wished it any other way.'

Holmes paused and looked around the room at the solemn faces of the distinguished men who sat opposite us. 'I am not a military man, gentlemen, but if the safety of our nation is in the hands of men such as Captain Blandy, then I have no fears that Britannia will ever succumb to the external forces of evil.'

*****

It was two weeks later that a letter arrived at our rooms. Holmes had been busying himself writing a new paper about accents and their inflections and fortunately had not fallen into one of his post-case lethargies.

The envelope, plain but of the finest quality, was addressed to Holmes and me, and my friend bade me open and read it.

Dear Mr Sherlock Holmes and Dr John Watson,

We are most pleased to be able to write and express our profound and eternal thanks for the great service you have rendered your country once again. We have been briefed upon the nefarious and horrible activities that transpired in our most esteemed service, and have no doubt as to the danger that faced us all.

Although we enjoy reading about your exploits, we know that on this occasion the matter must be kept from our subjects until such time long in the future when circumstances have changed for the better.

We would be most pleased if you would both join us at a date to be arranged for a more formal recognition of your actions.

With growing amazement, I read the note again, taking particular time to contemplate the signature: *VR.*

I looked up to find Holmes smiling. 'Well, Watson, despite my protests as to your literary style, it seems you have an admirer!'

Epilogue

It was some months before Holmes and I were to learn the full scale of the plot we had uncovered when we met again with Rear-Admiral James Caddington at the Admiralty building just off Marble Arch.

Acting on Holmes' instruction, a massive search had been undertaken of all ships significant to the defence of the British Isles and her colonies. Hidden explosives had been found on four more ships of the line. If used at a decisive moment, the sinking or disablement of these ships would have critically impaired the security of the Realm.

It would seem that the German military, which lagged many years behind our own in terms of naval power, had hatched a daring scheme to cripple the cornerstones of the British fleet and thus secure a military victory leading to the capitulation of the government of the United Kingdom in matters of sovereignty in numerous colonies around the Mediterranean. This would undoubtedly have altered the balance of power in Europe, and eventually led to catastrophic consequences for our country.

With the uncovering of the plot, the British government was able to make powerful and persuasive representations to the German ambassador and almost certainly prevent an escalation of military activity and intent for the foreseeable future.

The Strange Case of the Fountain of Blood

Our involvement in this queer little case began one morning in April of the year 1888. It was a balmy day and I had just returned from an invigorating walk to the Serpentine, where I had partaken of the opportunity for a swim. Refreshed, and feeling most satisfied with the world, I returned to our rooms to find Holmes poring over an article in *The Times*. The curtains were drawn and foul odours were emanating from several bubbling test tubes that my roommate was heating over his Bunsen burners.

I confess I was somewhat irked to find my senses so assailed and sullied after such a cleansing morning. 'Really, Holmes!' I expostulated. 'It is the most unhealthy atmosphere in here. I must open the curtains and windows so that we may benefit from some fresh air and clear these noxious fumes.'

My friend raised a commanding hand. 'Do not do so until I have completed this experiment. It will require no more than five minutes, and the results are quite crucial.' He waved me away from the window and I resigned myself to a few more moments of discomfort as I felt my eyes watering and my throat becoming parched.

My companion, to the contrary, appeared utterly unaffected by the poisonous humours he had created. He busied himself with the test tubes and chemicals while I sank into my chair holding a kerchief to my mouth as a token defence against the acrid stench.

Within a few moments, Mrs Hudson's voice could be discerned. Her most strident tone rang through the closed door. 'Mr Holmes! There is the most dreadful smell coming down the landing!'

Holmes grimaced and replied, 'One moment, I beg of you, Mrs Hudson, and all will be right. Aha! I thought so!'

He placed a tube containing a thick brownish liquid into a rack and rushed to the curtains. Parting them, he threw the window open so hard that I feared the panes would break before dashing to the other windows of our rooms and repeating his actions. Finally, he flung open our door and faced our irate housekeeper.

'My sincere apologies, Mrs Hudson.' Holmes immediately employed the special soothing voice he retained especially for her. 'I got a little carried away. I assure you that the gases are not harmful and will clear momentarily. In the meantime, I know both Watson and I would be most grateful for some of your delicious morning tea, perhaps with a slice of your excellent sponge cake.'

Mrs Hudson, still as susceptible as any of her sex to flattery, gave my friend a look of wry admonishment then turned with a theatrical huff and set off for the kitchen.

'Holmes, please tell me you have discovered the age-old secret of alchemy, for I declare my lungs will accept nothing less by way of compensation.'

For a moment I thought Holmes might laugh at my attempt at levity, but he quickly recovered his composure and stood staring out of the open window. 'Why red?' he mused aloud. 'Why not blue, or green, or violet?'

'I might be able to contribute if I had any notion as to what you were referring,' I replied.

'Hmm,' responded Holmes. He strode to the table and threw the newspaper that rested there across to me. I glanced at the front page but perceived nothing to which my friend's activities might be related. 'Page five,' urged Holmes impatiently.

I turned to the indicated page and my eyes alighted upon a most preposterous headline to a small story: *Blood Flows in the Streets of Town*. I raised my eyes to find my friend's eyes fixed upon me, so I cleared my throat and started to read aloud.

'*The market town of Hitchin is today centre of the wildest speculation as to the cause of the market fountain regularly running with blood between the hours of six in the evening and five in the morning. Local residents and shopkeepers can offer no explanation as to the most peculiar events that have transpired these past six days. Even though the local constabulary have looked into the matter, they have as yet been unable to trace the origin of the phenomenon.*'

The article went on to give some eyewitness accounts of the clear water suddenly turning red at the stated hour then just as rapidly reverting to purity some eleven hours later. The story concluded with the assertion that some local churchgoers were beginning to claim the occurrence as a divine sign.

'Most peculiar!' I exclaimed. 'Do you have any notion as to the cause?'

Holmes paused the pacing he had begun, which was always a sign of deep thought to which the threadbare rug bore testimony. 'I have some ideas and feel confident in ruling out any aspects of the divine or supernatural, but I must agree it is a most intriguing little conundrum. Therefore, I feel there is nothing for it but to take a short excursion. I would be most grateful if you would come along, Watson.'

As always I didn't hesitate. 'Why, I would be delighted, my dear Holmes. My diary is free for the afternoon and, as I recall, tomorrow is also vacant.'

Holmes spun on his heel. 'Then let us dally no longer. A cab to Liverpool Street and luncheon in Hitchin!'

*****

A short train journey of no more than an hour and a quarter brought us to the delightful town nestling in the North Hertfordshire countryside. Flowers of every conceivable hue greeted our arrival, and a short walk from the railway station found us in the town centre.

Holmes stopped and regarded the fountain that stood at the very heart of the market square for several minutes. It was a splendid example of a stonemason's art, standing perhaps a full nine-feet tall, and it had large troughs at three feet from the base that were fed by open funnels from above. The water ran crystal clear.

As we examined the structure, a drayman brought his two horses to it to slake their thirst. While the fine beasts were drinking their fill, Holmes turned to the man. 'I say, my good fellow, what do you know of this peculiar business with the fountain?' He spoke in a friendly tone that was often, as I had seen before, particularly effective at eliciting a response from the lower classes.

The man regarded us warily. 'You be tourists I s'pose? Or more o' them men from the press?' His disdain was apparent.

'I see you are too quick for us, my man! I had hoped to find a little local perspective,' said Holmes, a half guinea appearing in his right hand. He twirled it absently through his fingers to ensure it gained the drayman's full attention.

'Well, I don't know much, 'cept I can say that-there water is fine for both beast and man during daylight. I've been using this 'ere fount fer all my life, and never have I seen so much as a splash o' colour in it afore now.'

He hesitated, his eyes fixed upon the coin my friend was manipulating with all the skill of a conjurer. Holmes' long fingers were under perfect control as he urged the drayman to continue. 'Well, there was a time mebbe three week ago when I was 'ere with the horse when I did see it flow red for no more than a twinkling, but then it was clear again. I didn't think much of it. I thought best not to say n'more when this business started, lest other folks might think I was pretendin' or shoulda said afore now.'

Holmes regarded the man keenly. 'Do you happen to remember the time and the day?'

The drayman's brows furrowed then his eyes lit up. 'It was mornin', 'bout eleven, and a Wednesday. I remember now as my round takes me here at that time, but only on a Wednesday. And I'm sure it were three week ago.'

Holmes smiled briefly then said, 'Well, I don't see how that helps but I thank you for your time.' He flipped the coin to the fellow and bade him good day.

When we were alone I waited while Holmes gazed thoughtfully at the water gushing from the fountain. 'A shame the man could be no real help,' I ventured.

My colleague stared absently at me then mused, 'On the contrary, he was most helpful and has, I believe, set us upon the right path.' Suddenly energised, he spun on his heel and headed for the police station on the opposite side of the square.

I hurried to follow as Holmes strode in through the door and halted before the heavy oak counter. A constable was seated behind it, a mug of tea steaming at his right hand and a local newspaper open which he affected to read. He ignored both Holmes and I as we approached, and it was not until my friend rapped loudly on the countertop that we elicited any response.

'Yes, gentlemen?' the constable emphasised the words with a bored sarcasm.

'I wish to see your superintendent, and quickly,' Holmes said curtly.

'Oh you do, do you? The superintendent is very busy and doesn't take kindly to being disturbed.'

Carefully and deliberately, my companion placed his card directly before the constable on top of the newspaper.

The country constable's eyes widened. 'Mr Holmes! Mr Sherlock Holmes! I shall tell the super you are here. Please excuse me.'

He bustled away as Holmes turned and winked at me. 'Nice to see my name carries at least a little weight even in these parts.' I knew that my friend, for all his amazing abilities, was still susceptible to a little professional vanity on occasion.

Within moments the constable returned, followed by a florid man of near fifty years wearing a beaming smile and crumbs at his lips and in his moustache. The superintendent extended his hand and pumped my friend's vigorously. 'Mr Holmes, we are all keen students of your methods here in Hitchin. I must confess that I never thought to see you standing here in our station, though. It must be this little puzzle over the fountain. Am I right?'

Holmes smiled. 'I see you are a perceptive man, my good superintendent...?'

'Burroughs, Oswald Burroughs. How can we assist you? Do you have any leads?' It was obvious to me that the man had no clues, nor was likely to unearth any soon.

'It is early days, and this may well prove to be a long and complex investigation,' began the famous detective. 'And I am afraid that I have yet to form any hypotheses, having only been in your charming town for a half hour.' The officer's eyes fell. 'Anyhow, I should consider it a singular favour if you could spare a little time to show both myself and Dr Watson around the locality.'

The superintendent immediately perked up. 'It would be a pleasure. I might have a little time to spare right now, if that suits?'

'Splendid! Let us not tarry, for I am sure that a brisk walk might stimulate our faculties and then perhaps a solution might suggest itself,' proclaimed Holmes exuberantly.

I followed and we proceeded around the market square, the police officer pointing out some of the quaint little shops as well as the courthouse, the infirmary, the neat little town hall, the gaol and a little further distant, the local church. Holmes appeared interested, but try as I might, I could not perceive his intent.

After we had started up a side street, Holmes suddenly stopped in front of a standing tap. He reached down and cupped his hands to collect some of the clear water flowing from the faucet. 'Tell me, officer, has this tap ever flowed red as well?'

'Oh no, sir, that one is always clear, day and night. Matter of fact, that is the nearest one that is pure during the night time, and it is the water that the horses use in the evening. Is it a clue, Mr Holmes?' The superintendent looked nonplussed.

'You are a sharp man, officer, but it may be of no consequence. I take it that the town hall over yonder contains an archive of the civil engineering plans of the town? I should like to examine the designs for the sewerage and drainage of the market square and its environs.'

For a moment the superintendent appeared baffled but then he collected himself. 'I am sure the plans will be there but I don't think there will be anything to be learned from them. I personally looked them over yesterday.'

'I am sure you are right, superintendent, but to satisfy my own mind I would be very grateful if I might also be allowed a viewing.'

Ten minutes later we were standing in a high, oak-panelled room with three great leather-topped tables arranged in the centre. A clerk appeared carrying two roles of architects' paper, which he carefully spread out upon two of the sturdy tables. Immediately Holmes started to examine the drawings, his thin fingers dancing across the schematics of the central town area.

I wandered over to a large sash window and gazed over the town square from our second-floor vantage point. The scene was much as one would expect: draymen with their fine horses making deliveries to the public houses, wives clutching baskets containing the fruits of their custom at the numerous shops that occupied three sides of the quadrangle. Without a doubt the vista was startling only in that it was so ordinary. I wondered idly how many other towns across our land were just like this. Yet the presence of Holmes and myself in this most unremarkable community was a result of the most unusual events; scratch the surface and often things are not as they might first appear, I mused.

My reverie was cut short by a conversation between Holmes and our host. 'I have not been able to determine anything definite. However, I would very much like to inspect your little gaol as I have a keen interest in the facilities for holding the less-desirable elements of society.'

The police officer looked dubious, then brightened. 'It is irregular but as it is you, Mr Holmes, I don't think the magistrates would object.'

Our helpful superintendent accompanied us to the gaol house on the southern side of the market square. To my eyes, the building seemed older than many of the other premises in the vicinity, although I suspected that the façade had undergone a more recent refurbishment.

The superintendent addressed a guard seated just inside the heavily reinforced door. 'This here is Mr Sherlock Holmes and Dr Watson, visiting us from London. I should like to show them around.' The guard affirmed his agreement, casting my companion little more than a glance. It seemed that the detective's name was not one in which he had much interest.

Burroughs led us toward some offices that appeared to be inhabited. I could see silhouettes and hear raised voices through the frosted glass of the door as we approached. 'This is Constable Maddocks,' said the superintendent by way of introduction to a burly, uniformed policeman who appeared to be remonstrating with a sallow-faced skivvy who was cowering before him.

Maddocks looked none too pleased at being interrupted, but he composed himself rapidly and bade the man get back to work. 'Sorry 'bout that, sir. He burned the prisoner's food yet again, and mine also. He really has been quite slack since we took him on.'

The skivvy hurried past us and out of the room. Holmes glanced after him and then turned to the constable. 'How long has he been with you?' he asked.

'Not more than three weeks or so. Arrived here one afternoon and offered his services at a very fair price. Mind you, I'm beginning to think he's not worth it, no matter what the wage.'

Holmes smiled. 'Ah well, perhaps someone better will come along presently. I should be most grateful if you would show us the cells.'

'This-a-ways then, gentlemen. Mind, we don't have many in at the moment. Been quite peaceable 'round these parts of late.'

'Then the credit is yours, my good officers,' declared Holmes. 'Your force has undoubtedly withered the criminal will in this town.' The policemen shared a pleased smile, tinged, I perceived, with a certain smugness.

Our little band tripped down the stone stairs to the cells which lined the right side of a low and musty chamber made of old brick. A series of gas burners set at intervals along the left-hand wall provided the dim lighting. An unlit grate stood at one end and there was a constant drip of water, though from whence it came I could not discern.

I made a quick calculation and estimated there were at least ten cells but most appeared empty, as the constable had explained previously. However, three had residents and the constable described their misdemeanours as we passed.

'This 'ere is Wigham, he's a mucher. This one's Mitchell, he likes to take horses that don't belong to him, and this beauty is Williams. He's our prize lad doing three to five for a burglary at the Grange.' Williams was a surly-looking individual who gazed out malevolently from behind his bars.

Holmes dismissed the convicts with a wave of his hand. 'Well, I see that they are nicely tucked up here and I am sure the townsfolk are most grateful for your efforts. Come, Watson, I think it is time for us to head for the station. If we don't tarry, we will make the afternoon train back to London. Then tomorrow we must return with our mining expert.'

I was rather baffled by Holmes' last comment, but I freely admit that I was more than relieved to leave the confines of the prison. The light afternoon air was most agreeable as we stepped smartly from the gaol and back into the town square. Holmes drew the superintendent to one side and engaged him in a brief but earnest conversation. I was unable to hear the contents, but it concluded with the officer scurrying off in the direction of the station house at no mean lick.

As Holmes regained my side, I set out in the direction of the station only to be diverted from our course once we had left the square. Holmes took us down a side alley and we happened upon a small lodging house. 'We stay here for now,' he declared. 'We shall take supper, for there is a rum night's work ahead of us, Watson.'

I knew better than to press my friend for further explanation, accustomed as I had become to his methods. It was not until after we had finished our surprisingly good steak-and-kidney pie that Holmes leaned back and regarded me. 'This is a relatively simple case, but not without some points of interest. I fear, though, that we might be in for a rough night of it.'

I affirmed my readiness for action and Holmes continued. 'Anyhow, here comes the good superintendent now.' A scuff of footsteps could be heard and within moments the fellow was with us.

'I have it, Mr Holmes!' Burroughs carried a roll of draughtsman's paper under his arm. 'But I don't see what good it will do us as I am sure the engineer has already made an inspection.'

'That I don't doubt,' said my colleague. 'But he would almost certainly have been looking in the wrong place.'

Holmes pushed the remains of our meal aside and spread what appeared to me to be a large-scale drawing of the town's sanitation and water supply. His long fingers danced over the aged paper, almost seeming to sense their way rather than be guided. 'I have it! Here is where we shall find the solution to our little mystery.' He jabbed at a symbol that I took to portray a manhole cover.

A short walk of two hundred yards in the cool evening air saw us standing in a small alleyway to the south of the market square. Within minutes, we were joined by two more of Burroughs' men both carrying storm lanterns that could be shielded. The larger of the two men, the constable we had met earlier at the gaol house, advanced to the heavy iron cover at our feet and lifted it aside with a pair of manhole keys. Holmes put his fingers to his lips and one by one we carefully picked our way down an iron ladder into the darkness.

A lamp was handed down and I could see that Holmes and I were standing on a stone ledge some four feet wide. In a channel at our feet flowed the old watercourse that I surmised must supply the fountain.

When we had all assembled, Holmes checked his half hunter and whispered, 'It is now a quarter to six. We must hurry. Regardless of what you might hear, remain silent and still until I give word.' I could see the familiar steely resolve in his eyes as the yellow light of the two lamps threw eerie shadows on the old brick walls and arched ceiling.

We advanced cautiously and silently until we reached a sharp bend in the tunnel. Holmes held up his hand and we halted. At his bidding the covers on the lanterns were lowered and we were plunged into total darkness.

I am not a man given to fancy, but never have I experienced such a disconcertingly total absence of light. Truly, one could not see a hand an inch from one's face. In the darkness I was aware only of the gentle breathing of my companions and the constant burbling of the water as it ran in the channel. But we did not have to wait long until we heard footsteps and discerned a faint glimmer of light approaching from around the corner. There was a sound as if someone or something had entered the water and then a scraping sound could be clearly heard.

I know now that we remained as we were for more than four hours. My limbs were cold and aching, and in the gloom my imagination began to play games as I listened to the almost hypnotic scrape, scrape, scrape drifting down to us from ahead. Suddenly there was a crashing roar and I felt a hammer blow to my chest. I was aware of Holmes shouting, 'Now! Light!' Within an instant the tunnel was illuminated, and my friend leapt forward and around the bend. I sprang after him, followed closely by the policemen.

There was a splash and I saw Holmes grappling with a man in the water. I jumped in to assist and in moments we had the fellow held firm. I looked down to see our charge and recognised Williams, the burglar from the gaol. His body went limp as he realised that further struggle would be to no avail.

I looked up to see a huge hole blown in the side of the tunnel through which water was pouring. From ahead there were the sounds of a further struggle and then the voice of an officer, 'I have him, sir!'

A man I saw to be the skivvy was brought before us. In the half-light Holmes' thin face looked exultant. Drenched to the skin, we made our way back to the ladder and up into the night.

Half an hour later saw Holmes and I dried and garbed in heavy woollen greatcoats kindly provided by Burroughs, and enjoying a mug of thick, sweet tea back at the station house. Our clothes hung over racks in front of the crackling fire in the grate. Our two captives sat sullen faced, handcuffed to heavy chairs in the corner of the superintendent's office.

'Well, Watson, in all honesty I did not anticipate an evening dip when first we set out this morning,' said Holmes. 'I fear we may both suffer for it in the morning, though not as much as these two specimens.' He nodded at the two miscreants who glared at us with unconcealed hatred.

'Mr Holmes, you will kindly do us the favour of explaining exactly how you were able to see through this matter. I must have the details for my report,' entreated Burroughs.

'Indeed I shall, but first I would like it noted that I have no particular interest in receiving attention for this case. The reason shall become clear during my discourse.

'The problem was a pretty one, but I determined that the key to the mystery was the times at which the fountain ran red. Something had to be interfering with the water between the hours of six and five. If we discount the supernatural, which I invariably do, then we were left with a man-made influence. A man, or men, must be engaged in some activity at certain times to cause the effect.'

Holmes paused and glanced around to ensure he had our full attention. Both Burroughs and I were furiously scribbling in our notebooks, and I was surprised to see my friend flash a rare wry smile.

He continued. 'I could not determine any reason for anyone wishing for the populace of Hitchin to avoid using the fount. I therefore concluded that it was more likely that the reddening of the water supply was a by-product of other activities, and whatever was causing it must be upstream of the outlet.

'My next task was to determine from which direction the watercourse flowed. My instincts were aroused when it became clear that it flowed in close proximity to the cells under the police station. An escorted visit to the aforesaid place confirmed it, and I recognised the man you call Williams as a certain Robert Bennett, one of the nastiest and least desirable of London's ruffians.'

At this, Bennett snarled, 'Curse you and yours, Mr Sherlock Holmes!' No sooner had he spat his vehemence than Burroughs cuffed him soundly round the ear and he sat in sullen silence once more.

Holmes smiled thinly. 'Much to my chagrin, this fellow managed to give me the slip more than a year past. I am satisfied that this time I am the victor, and it is London and the Home Counties that shall benefit from his secure incarceration.

'By now I was convinced that the source of our problem was an intended gaolbreak, and that the reddening of the stream was caused by tunnelling through the red bricks and clay that imprisoned our friend here. Further, the time of the aberration was critical; he could only safely work on his escape overnight while the guard was tucked up in his office.

'I immediately recognised Bennett, even though he turned and shrank away from me. However, I gave no sign of my recognition but instead used the opportunity to declare in a loud voice that I would be returning with a mining expert the following day. This immediately alerted Bennett to the fact that I was intending to investigate below ground, so he had little choice but to complete his tunnel and make his escape that night. I forced his hand, and you gentlemen were there to experience the result.

'This man,' Holmes gestured toward the cook, 'was Bennett's accomplice in a number of his nefarious activities. Once Bennett had been tried, it was he who immediately began work to free his friend. By taking the role of cook at the gaol house, he could smuggle tools to his partner and work on the tunnel from the other side. By foiling this escape,' Holmes turned to Burroughs, 'you have successfully brought two desperate felons to justice and undoubtedly prevented a great number of further crimes that the two would have engaged upon within days of a successful escape.'

'But Mr Holmes,' began the honest superintendent, 'the credit is yours. I can hardly claim to have solved the mystery.'

Holmes held up a hand. 'Nonsense! It was your readiness to act decisively that bought this matter to a positive resolution. Besides, I was dissatisfied that this man eluded me a year ago. I have no wish to revisit that failure in the local and national press.

'Now, I think it is time that Watson and I returned to the relative peace of our great capital. I think the countryside is sometimes a little lively for our demeanours.' Holmes chuckled at his joke and I found myself smiling as we departed for the promise of a fine breakfast at the Metropole – provided we made the early train.

The Adventure of the Creature in Stone

The last time Mr Sherlock Holmes and I had holidayed together, there had been the ghastly business of the Devil's Foot. My friend was not a man who generally enjoyed departing our great city, preferring the bustle and energy of the capital to the quieter, more sedate life of the countryside.

On more than one occasion, however, my colleague had intimated darkly that there was just as much crime of the most terrible and depraved kind away from the sprawling buildings and streets of the largest conurbation in the world. He had noted that the remoteness and privacy afforded by the less-densely populated areas of our isle could harbour and give shelter to the most barbarous of killers, or the most ingenious of criminals.

But Sherlock Holmes' natural habitat was London. Here he sat at the centre of an intelligence-gathering web composed of all levels of society, from the young street urchins whose sharp eyes missed little to the civil servants whose machinations ran our country.

So it was with surprise that, as we breakfasted one morning, I heard Holmes utter the words, 'Watson, I think it is time I took a holiday. Would you be so good as to accompany me as my travelling companion?'

I nearly choked on the devilled egg Mrs Hudson had provided and looked up to see my friend regarding me with an amused twinkle in his eye. 'What ho, Watson! Did I catch you unawares?'

I replied that he most certainly had, but that I would be most glad to gain a week or two away from the ever-present activity of the city and would enjoy a quiet sojourn and some clean air. 'Then let us waste no time. We should be able to make the ten thirty-five from Paddington.'

I began to protest that I had to arrange cover for my practice and to pack, but once Holmes' mind was made up he would brook no dispute. After sending a telegram to Dr Worthington, who often covered for me when matters took me away from my work, and hastily packing a valise, I soon found myself at the great railway station still none the wiser as to our ultimate destination.

I had endeavoured to ask Holmes as to where we might be holidaying while our hansom tripped over the cobbles but he had simply bade me quiet and sat with his eyes closed and a look of surprising contentment upon his countenance. Indeed, he looked in ruder health than I had seen him in a long time, so I was happy to let him have his little mystery.

As we waited on the platform and the majestic locomotive began to breathe smoke more urgently as the driver and fireman coaxed the marvel to life, a small boy approached my friend. Without saying a word, he slipped a piece of folded paper into Holmes' hand. It was deftly done, and the only reason I saw it was because I was not unfamiliar with the great detective's methods. After the 'drop', as Holmes would call such a delivery, I was about to speak when he fixed me with his cool gaze and I decided to wait.

It was not until more than a half hour later, as we were hurtling away from London at a speed I estimated to be in excess of sixty miles per hour, that Holmes spoke. 'I suppose you must be curious as to that little episode on the platform.'

I agreed that I was.

'My dear Watson, we are indeed taking a break from the city and shall be holidaying in the Isle of Wight, but there is a small matter I may look into while we are there.'

Much as I craved the tranquillity of a rural retreat, I must admit that my interest was immediately piqued and I leaned forward eagerly. To my amazement, Holmes grinned wickedly. 'Watson, I knew I could count on you as always. Your very predictableness is one of your most endearing features.' He reached into his coat pocket and withdrew a letter, which he passed to me.

My Dear Holmes,

I write to you concerning a matter which is vexing me most severely. As you may know, I have recently been engaged by the new Natural History Museum of Kensington as a research fellow. My work upon the petrified remains of the great beasts that once roamed our earth has gained particular attention from the scientific establishment of late, and the amazing finds that I have made in the Isle of Wight have afforded considerable new insight into the prehistory of our land.

However, it is becoming very apparent to me that there are those who do not welcome the discoveries I am making, and matters came to a head last week with an grievous attack upon my work and even a physical assault upon my person.

I implore you, as a friend, to help me in these dark times and to journey here to Ventnor so that these heinous crimes may be curtailed and those responsible brought to account.

Yours Faithfully,
Nathaniel Drake (Dr)

I looked up to find Holmes gazing abstractedly out of the window at the Hampshire scenery rushing past. 'I wasn't aware that you were a friend to Dr Drake,' I said.

Holmes waved it away as of little importance. 'He and I roomed together for a short while many years ago.'

I was immediately intrigued as Holmes rarely mentioned his formative years. To my frustration, my companion was not forthcoming so I decided to probe a little further. 'Was he as brilliant then as his reputation suggests now?'

Holmes coughed. 'He was a man of considerable imagination,' that was certainly a rebuff by Holmes' standards, 'but was on occasion able to provide unexpected insight into his field of study.'

I realised that pre-history was perhaps as important to Holmes as studies in the supernatural. I have noticed and commented on many occasions that his knowledge, while formidable and encyclopaedic on a wide range of matters, was restricted generally to areas that he considered relevant to his profession. He had held forth on the importance of not cluttering his mind with unnecessary and extraneous information, and chided me on my small interests in things more ephemeral. And those were the last words I heard from Sherlock Holmes, for he settled back in his seat and closed his eyes.

I spent the remainder of the journey thinking upon the reception we faced. I could feel the familiar surge of excitement that accompanied me on all of our adventures. I watched the countryside; I attempted to read a paper and gave up, and I was extremely relieved when finally we drew into Portsmouth to make the change for the ferry across to the island.

*****

Upon embarking Holmes and I ventured up to the top deck and stood there alone, drinking in the salted air and the crisp breeze of that April morning. The white chalk cliffs of our destination were clearly visible and grew as we slowly traversed the Solent. I inhaled deeply and savoured the scent of the sea. Although an army man, I have always found the sea an attraction, as do so many of our island race. Years earlier I had enjoyed a short holiday on the island with my dear Mary before she passed, and so I felt a sense of attachment to the place that was particularly private to me.

Holmes and I stood alone at the railing, lost in our own thoughts, for the ferry was mostly empty on this passage.

At the same instant we both became aware of rapid footsteps approaching us from behind. Instinctively I spun around and received a stunning blow across my temples. The sea, air, ferry and Holmes span and were immediately replaced by blackness as I lost consciousness.

I came to and found Holmes still unconscious beside me, a trickle of blood meandering from a cut above his left eye. I immediately started to bring him round, and within moments my friend's eyes opened. After a second or two they focused and locked on to me. 'Holmes, can you hear me?' I cried.

'Perfectly, thank you, Watson, and I should consider it a mercy if you shouldn't shout so in my ear.' Holmes sat upright and then stood a little shakily, dusting off his frock coat as he did so. I also rose to my feet and, leaning on the safety railing, regarding my friend. His face was pale but the colour was returning to his sallow cheeks.

'Obviously we are not welcome,' I observed dryly.

My companion gave a slight grimace as he dabbed at his wound with a kerchief. 'It was only meant to provide a scare. They could easily have killed us or thrown us over the side and left us to drown. No, it really won't do! I... Hello, what's this?' As he was speaking Holmes had thrust his hands into his coat pocket, for although the sun was bright the air had a nip to it. Now he withdrew his right hand clutching an envelope. With deft fingers he opened it and withdrew a piece of parchment. He held it up and read aloud:

Mr Holmes and Mr Watson.

You are not welcome here. Your attempts to resolve the matters presented to you by Dr Drake will only endanger your wellbeing further.

Consider this a final warning.

'Come, Watson, there is not a moment to lose if we are to apprehend the scoundrels before we dock.' And with that we both made haste to the departure door, reaching it as the ferry drew alongside the dock.

Holmes and I were the first to disembark. No sooner had our shoes touched land than my companion was hurrying me to take refuge behind a stack of crates piled up on the quayside. From our vantage point we observed the departure of our fellow passengers, none of whom appeared to me to be likely candidates. Holmes, however, appeared satisfied.

Once the last person had crossed the gangplank and made their way past the waiting stewards, I felt a tug at my sleeve. I hurried after Holmes toward a waiting dogcart whose driver was holding a card with my friend's name upon it. 'Did you see the rogues?' I asked as soon as we were on our way.

'No, Watson, I did not – which confirmed my suspicions. I know who they are and can lay my hands upon them as soon as I need to.'

My mouth opened and I tried to press him further but was cut short before I could speak. 'Not now, there's a good chap. I need to think.' We sat in silence for the remainder of the journey, I nursing a growing bump upon my head and Holmes staring abstractedly toward the horizon.

It was nearly an hour later that we pulled up outside a dark red-brick building with a steeply gabled roof some quarter of a mile from Ventnor. The property stood alone and looked solid enough, but would have benefited from a new coat of paint on its peeling window frames. Holmes and I alighted and, after thanking the driver, hurried to knock at the heavy wooden double door. Presently it was opened by a man of smallish stature who ushered us inside and then peered out nervously and furtively.

'Holmes!' he exclaimed, slamming the door and locking it. 'Sherlock Holmes!' He pumped my friend's hand so vigorously that I began to fear for his state of mind.

'Dr Drake, please allow me to introduce Dr Watson, my colleague and friend. I do not doubt that his presence will prove invaluable during our stay.'

Dr Nathaniel Drake was a man of considerable presence despite his diminutive size. His quick blue eyes moved rapidly from one of us to the other and he exuded a sense of energetic determination. His greying hair was unkempt and longer than the fashion, and his worn apron hid a coat that appeared even more distressed than his overalls. He fulfilled my image of a researching scientist in the field most admirably.

I gazed around the large workshop-cum-laboratory in which we stood. Everywhere were rocks of all sizes, many split open to reveal the curious remains of bestial creatures, often twisted into obscene poses or existing only as fragments of their once-terrible forms. Over to my right was a series of benches with a massive incomplete skeleton laid upon them, each bone carefully labelled and placed in relation to the rest. Stacked against a wall were large jars, each containing acids and strong alkali solutions I recognised from my undergraduate days.

Dr Drake urged us to a small area that had been set out with a pair of threadbare sofas and some tub chairs. Once we were seated, the poor fellow began to crumble before our eyes. 'Oh, Mr Holmes, what shall I do? Only this morning my assistant, Babcock, left me saying he could stand no more. He had, I am convinced, only stayed this long out of concern for my welfare. But he has a young wife and child and I cannot expect him to run the risks that I do. He has promised to return the day after the morrow to collect his things and check on me. I know he will try to persuade me to return to London, but I must not lose my resolve. My work is here, and the progress I am making is of such profundity that I must face the danger, no matter if it means my life.'

Holmes reached out and touched the man's arm. I have on occasion seen Holmes employ this method of quieting a troubled soul. 'Nathaniel, please try to give us the facts of the matter from the very beginning, if you would. I urge you to include even the smallest detail you can recall.' He spoke earnestly and gently, and immediately I saw Dr Drake begin to calm.

The scientist took a deep breath and began in a carefully measured tone, 'I first came to the island six weeks ago in response to a find made by a local schoolteacher and keen amateur named Merriweather. The tides had been particularly strong and had revealed a most impressive Ichthyosaur embedded in the undercliff near St Catherine's Point. Such a find is extremely rare, so I hurried here to begin the retrieval before damage was done to the remains.'

'Damage?' enquired Holmes.

'Certainly. The seas can be rough around these parts and the cliffs are prone to erosion, not to mention local interest! I did not want the schoolchildren of the island hacking away at it with who knows what implements. Upon arrival, my assistant and I immediately began the work of removing the creature and packing it in plaster for later preparation and study. However, it was not long before we began to realise that our presence here was unwelcome in some quarters.'

At this point Dr Drake paused, clearly troubled. Holmes and I waited patiently while he gathered himself. 'Both Babcock and I received letters warning us off the island. They were most disturbing but as the days passed my resolve hardened. Despite entreaties from my assistant, who was most touchingly concerned for my safety, I was resolute. The finds here are of such importance that I was determined not to be diverted from my work.'

He reached over to a drawer and withdrew an envelope. It appeared to my eyes to be the same as the one that Holmes had discovered in his pocket after our assault. I was just about to say so when Holmes caught my eye, and

I immediately perceived his desire that I keep my observation to myself.

It was written in a neat and legible hand, certainly the same hand as the letter planted on Holmes at the ferry. My colleague read aloud:

Dr Drake,

If you value your life, and the lives of those about you, you must quit the island now and forever. If you should not, the foulest conjurings of your imagination will not approach the danger which you and your accomplices will face for as long as you remain.

Be assured that your lives are in the gravest of danger, and the deaths you shall meet will be most brutal and visceral.

'It is unsigned. Most illuminating. Most illuminating indeed,' said Holmes.

I must say that the blank expression on Dr Drake's face confirmed to me that he had little more understanding of the significance than I, though I am sure we were both in accord that never had we heard such a dreadful missive.

'Pray continue, Dr Drake,' urged the detective.

'At that instance, I was angry. I am not a man to be bullied, although I'll admit my resolve has been most sorely tested since then. I rebuffed my assistant's entreaties and determined that we should press on with the excavation regardless. Nothing happened for the next two weeks, and I began to feel that the menace had receded. How wrong I was, Sherlock! It was then that an attempt was made upon the life of my assistant as he journeyed to the nearby store for provisions. The poor man was hurrying along when he heard the crack of a rifle shot, followed by two more in rapid succession. Instinctively he dived for the cover of a nearby wall, his training in the 43rd Light serving him well. He remained there for a good quarter of an hour before summoning his courage and wits and making a run it.'

'Was any other person with him when this attempt was made?' asked Holmes.

'No, sir, he was alone. But he had the presence of mind to return and remove these from the wall.' Dr Drake rose and, pulling down an old tobacco tin, removed from it three flattened bullets which he handed to my friend. Holmes subjected them to one of his most detailed inspections and pronounced himself satisfied.

'I assume that the fire you suffered last Tuesday past was no more than another inconvenience and was rapidly extinguished?' Holmes said, gazing absently at the ceiling.

'How did you know about that? I have told not a living soul. It was frightening, not because of the damage but because it made me realise that we could so easily have been consumed. It was then that I decided to write to you, Holmes.'

'But surely you have called in the local constabulary? Have they not been able to assist you?'

'There is a local detective inspector by the name of Oswelstry, the only one on the island, so I am led to believe. He has failed to shed any light on the matter and confided in me that he felt that for my safety I should leave, at least until the matter is resolved. But still, you have not told me how you knew of the fire!'

'Oh, it was a simple matter. I observed upon entering that there was a blackened patch of soot in the far left corner of your roof. It is hardly visible from the outside. Since there is no stove beneath, I surmised that the source had to be something else. Further, I noted that the soot appeared fresh and no cobwebs had formed over it, therefore it must have happened in the past few days. I concluded that it had been the most recent distressing occurrence, and that it was likely to have caused you to write me the letter requesting I lend my assistance. As it is now a Thursday and the letter you sent was postmarked yesterday, I suggest that you sent the letter after a sleepless night on Tuesday.'

'Astounding! Correct on all counts! Holmes, I have no doubt that you are the man to bring these matters to a satisfactory conclusion.'

'On the contrary, I believe I already have the solution to this little puzzle. I would like to take some supper and retire for the night. Tomorrow we must visit your excavation at first light, for I fear the final answers to our little mystery are to be found there. Tonight we must take turns at keeping a vigil, for those that threaten us may avail themselves of the opportunity to take decisive action now that we three are under the same roof.'

Dr Drake elected to take the first watch and, fortified by strong coffee, he sat in a chair we had placed by the door. I was to take the second shift and Holmes the third. Feeling somewhat fatigued from the long day's travelling,

I settled down on the sofa with an old blanket drawn across me, while Holmes slept in an easy chair, his narrow feet upon an old footstool.

Both Dr Drake's watch and my own passed without event. It was not until past five in the morning that I was stirred by Holmes briskly shaking my shoulder. Immediately I was awake and Holmes put his finger to his lips signalling quiet. Noiselessly we walked on tiptoe toward the door. We were both still a full five yards away, but faint sounds could be heard from without.

I was just reaching for the heavy wooden mallet I had identified earlier as a useful weapon when a great explosion blew the door from its hinges. The next few moments were a blur, but I saw Sherlock Holmes dash through the shattered doorway and out into the night. Struggling to my feet, I set off on his heels as fast as I could and caught up with him perhaps a half a minute later. He had stopped by a low stone wall and was looking around. Of our quarry, there was no sign.

I uttered an oath and Holmes spoke grimly. 'No matter, Watson. We will have our man before the morning is out.' With that, he strode swiftly back to our temporary abode.

Poor Dr Drake was standing in front of his workshop in obvious distress. 'Thank the stars you are both alive!' was his greeting upon seeing us. 'I thought that there could be nothing less than mortal injury from such an attack.'

'Dr Drake, we should barricade the doorway, take some breakfast, then visit the excavation. I believe that matters will be drawn to a satisfactory conclusion there,' said Holmes crisply.

*****

In truth, I was not in the least inclined to eat, but Holmes insisted that we should. After a hurried breakfast of ham and eggs, we wrapped ourselves in greatcoats and woollens and set off for the twenty-minute walk to the ichthyosaur site.

After a few minutes, we reached the post office in Ventnor. The postmaster was already opening up for the day and I observed a most bizarre charade acted out by my friend. He greeted the postmaster most jovially and asked to purchase a dozen envelopes. Holmes steered the man into the shop and re-emerged a few moments later clutching the stationery, which he made a point of showing to both Dr Drake and me. Knowing his methods, I went along with this little exhibition. Dr Drake, though clearly bemused, followed our lead.

We resumed our journey and before long were carefully climbing down the steep wooden staircase set in the side of the undercliff. Holmes, usually light and agile on his feet, seemed to be taking an unusually long time to make his descent and it was a full ten minutes before we stood together upon the shingle. I was concerned to see that Holmes appeared to be struggling for breath, although he waved away my attentions, and we made slow progress for the final fifty yards up the beach toward the dig.

I will admit now to a sense of disappointment. I had expected to see an impressive creature preserved in the cliffs; Instead, I saw little except for evidence of a lot of scraping and excavation. The sea was the master of this place and all along the cliff line was evidence of recent falls and erosion.

As we stood gazing at the scene of the discovery, I became aware of a figure on the cliffs above us. Suddenly there was a loud report, followed by the horrifying sight of the top section of the cliff coming away and crashing toward us. Holmes, miraculously recovering from his breathlessness, roughly pushed both Drake and I from harm's way and then was off at top speed, racing over the shingle back toward the wooden steps. After a moment I set off in pursuit, Dr Drake some distance behind but gallantly determined to play a part in the apprehension of the assailant.

Despite no longer being in the first flush of youth, never have I seen Holmes cover ground so fast. I realised that although he had intended to give the impression that he was out of condition and short of breath, he had been purposefully deep-breathing and flooding his muscles with oxygen in anticipation of the flight to come. He sprang up the steps two, three at a time and by the time I reached the top of the cliff he was waiting for me. Two constables and a burly plainclothesman were also in attendance. Held tightly between the two officers was a younger man of perhaps no more than thirty years. His head was slumped forward and a vivid bruise was developing above his right eye. He was, though, quite conscious and gazed at me belligerently.

Dr Drake called out as he mounted the last of the steps and hurried toward us. The constables and their man still had their backs toward him. 'Did you get the fiend?' the scientist gasped, but as he reached us he froze, his face a picture of bewilderment as he recognised the prisoner. 'Babcock! What are you doing here?' He turned to face Holmes. 'What is the meaning of this? Babcock here is my assistant. I was expecting him back today for his things.'

'He is also your mysterious assailant,' replied Holmes evenly. He turned to the plain-clothes policeman. 'Oswelstry, I think we should return to Dr Drake's quarters. I would be grateful if your men would bring Babcock along. I think we would all be more comfortable there while we discuss this matter further.'

*****

It was not long before we were all divested of our coats and assembled in the workshop. Babcock was seated, his wrists cuffed and a sullen expression on his countenance. The two constables standing immediately behind him remained alert and watchful.

'Holmes, you really must explain the meaning of this! What has Babcock to do with these matters?' Drake was bewildered and highly agitated.

Holmes turned slowly to face the miscreant and began. 'You will no doubt be aware that there are many in our society who do not welcome the notion that we are all descended from the great apes. Neither do they accept that the earth is more ancient than previously believed, and terrible creatures roamed our world long before the appearance of man. To many, such ideas are dangerous beyond belief. They threaten the very cornerstone of our civilisation and they are in direct contradiction to the teachings of many of the world's great religions. I immediately perceived that you, Dr Drake, were a very visible and successful proponent of this new thinking and therefore presented a most visible target for those who wish to persuade science away from this most contentious field of study.

'On the ferry, we were assaulted by persons unknown. In fact, they were sailors paid by Babcock to carry out the attack. They must have been given their orders in advance, therefore the person who planned the deed was aware that we were coming. However, their intent was to scare us, otherwise we would have been cast over the side to drown. The letter left upon me,' he passed it to Dr Drake who, after quickly scanning it, handed it to the inspector, 'was written upon a quality paper and placed in a quality envelope. The hand was legible and, although succinct, it was correct in its grammar. It was also written upon the same paper as the one you had received here, Dr Drake. I confirmed only this morning that the stationery could be purchased at the local postal office, where I also took the opportunity to send a message to the good inspector here. Fortunately for me, he is a man of action and took immediate steps to apprehend the criminal.'

Oswelstry visibly glowed under my friend's praise. 'Glad we could 'elp. Not so often we get such excitement down 'ere, Mr Holmes,' he proclaimed.

Holmes continued. 'I noted that Babcock was absent. By your own account, he had repeatedly tried to persuade you to leave the island. You further confirmed my suspicions when you told me of the attempted shooting of your assistant. The fact that there were no witnesses was strange. The idea that all three bullets would be recovered was also highly unlikely. But it was the bullets you provided that confirmed my suspicions. They had not been embedded in a wall because they bore no traces of cement or stone. The bullets had been purposefully hammered flat. I deduced, therefore, that Babcock desired to mislead you and to apply further coercion to make you leave the island. The fire and the explosion were all intended to intimidate, not to kill, but any one of these acts could have proved fatal if luck had been against us. Causing the cliff to fall upon us was a last act of desperation, but I was expecting something like it and so was alert and ready to act.'

'But why would he do this? Why? He is a scientist like me,' Dr Drake wailed. It was clear he was deeply upset.

'Why don't we ask him?' replied Holmes. Turning to the prisoner, he said, 'Speak up, man, for you are facing most serious charges. If, as I believe, you feel you have a cause that supports you then now is the time to make it known.'

Babcock stared at us and then spoke with quiet defiance. 'I recently became aware of the danger of some of these new discoveries that are being made in the name of science. They challenge the known wisdom of the ages and threaten to rend in two the very fabric of our society. I began to question my involvement in such endeavours and attended some meetings while in London. The people I met with also disagreed with such work and were determined to fight bravely to defend their beliefs and guide our troubled world back to the true path of enlightenment. I agreed to join them in their battle.'

He looked at each of us in turn, his gaze steady. 'I have no regrets.'

*****

Later, as Holmes and I were sitting in our Baker Street rooms, I with a cigar and Holmes with one of his favourite briars, we received word from Oswelstry. I listened with horror as Holmes related that Babcock had taken his own life whilst in custody. He had used the bed sheets from his cell to hang himself within hours of being charged.

Holmes was silent for a moment and then spoke with great sadness in his voice. 'I must confess I suspected something such as this might occur, and before we departed I urged Oswelstry to maintain a watch upon Babcock. When a man is so entrenched in his beliefs, and evidence to the contrary threatens all that he holds dear, such terrible inner conflict takes place as to make the most hideous of outcomes a likelihood.'

Deeply troubled, I nodded sombrely and tried to settle down to the papers.

The Horrible Case of the Burning Men

Part One

During my many years of intimate acquaintance with Sherlock Holmes, I was fortunate enough to join his investigations into many seemingly impenetrable mysteries. Indeed, I have commented on numerous occasions about his inhuman ability to perceive light where others see only darkness.

His unique talents have enabled him to dissect a problem in such a way as to make the solution appear almost unavoidable. However, there are few cases in which I have been so truly amazed by his ability to make the most astounding intellectual leaps, to arrive at a conclusion that might see the right man at the wrong end of a rope, as this one.

This case, the details of which were kept largely from public attention at the time in order to avoid hysteria and spare those involved from national disgrace, is one of those examples of my friend's quite extraordinary powers of reasoning.

It was a humid mid-summer afternoon. The city was frequently stifling and open windows provided little respite from the heavy blanket of heat that had settled over the capital. Our lives had been devoid of much excitement for a good two weeks or more, save for my regular sorties in search of an ice cream. Holmes, I was pleased to note, had not slipped into his usual lethargy, nor had he partaken of those substances I so abhor, but had busied himself by sorting and organising a vast stack of papers and reference material he had accumulated over the past several months. Indeed, I could hardly recall when I had last seen him so at ease between cases. It made a most agreeable change from the often morose man who emerged when there was little to excite his faculties.

Once in a while he would glance up from what he was reading and regale me with a detail from a scandal or a particularly revolting fact from a hideous murder in some faraway place. I had long been amazed that Holmes had a network that extended almost to the four corners of the globe; he had operatives working on his behalf who would clip interesting news stories or forward unusual court reports from both the old world and the new. Such information was not only essential to Holmes' continual development of his vast knowledge of sensational crime, but was also sweet nectar to his often starving mind.

Presently I became aware of voices and footfalls on the stairs outside our rooms. I glanced up to see that Holmes had similarly perceived them and while I could make out no words Holmes put his finger to his lips, raised an eyebrow and whispered, 'French.' He would later inform me that he can often discern a language from nothing more than a murmur by listening to its rhythm and tone.

But now I could hear the crisp voice of our housekeeper, immediately followed by a rap at the door.

'Come,' commanded my friend, and the door was thrown open to reveal Mrs Hudson, a most disapproving expression upon her countenance.

'This is Mr Grimaud,' she said and then, almost by way of explanation and to make her disdain obvious, 'he's French.'

Holmes bounded from his place at the table, a most uncharacteristic smile upon his lips. 'Philippe! Come in, my dear fellow!' Then turning to me, 'Watson, may I present Inspecteur Grimaud of the Sûreté Nationale.'

I stood and offered my hand which was accepted warmly. I had no doubt whatsoever that Holmes held the man in high regard for rarely have I ever seen him so enthusiastic in a greeting.

The tall and well-groomed man bowed as he shook my hand, his piercing green eyes never leaving my face for an instant. I could easily discern a formidable intelligence coupled, I suspected, with a single-minded determination. Without doubt, it was a certain presence that Holmes himself also had. Indeed, physically the two men had some similarity but where Holmes was dark, this man was much lighter in complexion and hair colour.

Of course, I had long been aware that Holmes tended to admire men who were of a similar disposition to himself, a trait that could easily be considered a conceit. But to Holmes it was merely a reflection of the importance he placed upon reason and his contempt for a lack of it in others.

My friend bade our visitor take a seat and drew up another with an entreaty to Mrs Hudson to provide refreshment at her earliest convenience. As soon as she had bustled off, Holmes became grave, a concerned frown lingering at her lips.

'I assume you are here on a professional matter, Inspecteur. No, don't tell me,' he held up his thin hand, 'it is the three charred corpses that have been recovered most recently from the Seine.'

'You are, of course, correct, Monsieur Holmes,' responded our guest in a quietly authoritative voice. If he was surprised by Holmes's deduction, he gave no sign of it. 'I have made some progress in the case, but have so far been unable to ascertain method or culprit.'

'You have, therefore, gained some insight as to motive?'

'A little. The victims are all successful businessmen; moreover, they are members of a society of financiers and venture capitalists. It is my belief that the murderer – for I am convinced that this *is* murder – is either a rival or a previous colleague bent upon revenge.'

'Then surely it is a matter of ascertaining who may gain from the demise of these men, or who may consider that they have been wronged by them in the past?' suggested Holmes.

'The society exists internationally and is very private and informal. There was only one complete directory of members, and there are no detailed records of past activity. Many members are familiar only with a few others, and may know only one or two of their brethren by name. You will understand that the men I have managed to interview are extremely unforthcoming about their business activities, and they refuse to speculate upon the activities of fellow members. This has so far rendered it impossible to make any significant advancement toward identifying possible suspects.'

A knock at the door signalled that Mrs Hudson had returned with some of her excellent cake and freshly brewed tea. I rose to my feet and bade our housekeeper hand the tray to me and ensure that we receive no visitors for the next hour or so.

After I had furnished my companions with our housekeeper's wares, Holmes continued. 'You mentioned that there was one directory of members. I note from your use of the past tense that this no longer exists?'

'Oh no, I am sure it exists. However, it is now in the hands of the perpetrator. You see, Monsieur Holmes, the holder of the list, a certain Monsieur Romuel, was the first to die. His charred remains were found some weeks ago lying by a roadside in a quiet suburb of our great capital. What you don't yet know is that the three recently recovered cadavers are not the first of their kind.'

Holmes looked up sharply. 'How many others Philippe?'

'At this present point in time,' our guest hesitated, 'I think at least six.'

'Great Heavens!' I exclaimed. 'How could so many distinguished men be slain without arousing immediate suspicion?'

'You must consider, Monsieur Watson, that these men were generally not well known. They were men who by choice were very private and shunned publicity in all its forms. Further, France is a large country and these men were spread out to the extremities of the republic. Finally, all have died within the last two months, a short timescale for pertinent information to find its way to someone who could discern a commonality to the deaths.

'But you have managed to reconstruct at least part of the directory, haven't you, Philippe?' said Holmes quietly.

'*Oui*. By a variety of means I have been able to discern some of the other possible members of the society. By deduction, analysis of correspondence, interviews with non-member colleagues and other means, I have created a list of men who may be members. It is by no means accurate or complete, but I am convinced that all the French members have been slain and that the murderer will now turn his attention to the British contingent.'

'Why do you believe that the British members will be next in turn for the attentions of our assassin? Why not denizens of any other country if the society is truly international?' asked Holmes.

'For the very reason that the last of the three men pulled from the Seine was an English businessman by the name of Appleton who was visiting Paris. He was almost certainly a member of the society. I had come upon his name from two other related sources.

'There is, though, a complication. In the course of my investigations I have happened upon certain information suggesting that while many of the society's dealings were of an entirely legal and proper nature, there were some that could be viewed as less than honourable. He paused, 'And without doubt, a number of them would result in the most severe ramifications for those involved.'

'Therefore, many of these men we would seek to protect would never admit to being involved in such a society,' mused Holmes. 'May I see the list, old friend?'

Without a word, our guest reached into his pocket and withdrew a single folded sheet of paper. He passed it to Holmes, who unfolded it and carefully read the contents. When he had finished he looked grim. 'I see the problem,' he said and handed me the paper.

A cursory glance told me that there were at least a dozen names on the list. But it was as I began to read that I felt the colour drain from my cheeks. Amongst the names I had never heard of were three with which I was most familiar. Indeed, the trio were names that would have been familiar to any Englishman, such were their elevated positions in our society.

'This is a pretty problem,' said Holmes. 'To protect these men, we must accuse them of being involved in a society and having dealings to which they could not possibly admit. Indeed, it is worse! In order to successfully investigate this matter, we ourselves would have to become aware of details that would almost certainly result in the ruin of these men. Besides, we do not yet know the murderer's modus operandi and who his next victim may be.'

'I might be able to assist there, Monsieur Holmes,' said our guest. 'I believe he is very systematic in his exterminations. So far, I am convinced that the villain has killed his victims in alphabetical order by surname. He is working his way through his list with absolute ruthlessness and precision.'

'I say, Holmes,' I ventured, 'surely we should inform our police of the situation at the earliest opportunity, lest we might be accused of hampering any investigation they might make.'

My friend turned to me and his gaze met mine. 'Ordinarily I would agree, Watson, but this is such a delicate situation that I fear such a disclosure would almost certainly make a bad situation far worse. Those whom we must seek to protect would be even less inclined to speak to the authorities. Within hours the pressmen would be on the scent and the immediate scandal that would ensue would be so damaging as to be almost beyond parallel.

'At this point in time, no crime has been committed on British soil. We have been approached by an internationally respected French official who will, I am sure, vouchsafe for us should circumstances require it. No, Watson, I see no alternative but to pursue this matter clandestinely for the moment.'

He turned to Inspecteur Grimaud. 'Philippe, of course, you cannot be seen here or to be involved operating in connection with this affair without the knowledge of Scotland Yard. May I suggest that you spend the evening furnishing me with all the details you can, then return to France tomorrow to continue your investigations. We will remain in contact by telegram. Be assured that I will summon you if necessary, and shall keep you apprised of all salient developments.'

Holmes and Grimaud spoke long into the night while I returned to my practice and made arrangements for a colleague to attend to my appointments for the next few days. In truth, I slept only fitfully that eve; my mind would not allow me the sanctuary of sleep so disturbed was I by the information to which I was privy.

*****

I returned to 221B Baker Street early the next morning and found Holmes in a sombre mood but ready to depart. 'This is a case that is not without its difficulties,' he confided. 'I am not confident of an amenable reception at our first meeting this morning.'

He hailed a hansom and we climbed aboard. 'Watson, there may be a point this morning at which I call upon you to stand fast in the face of considerable tribulations.'

I set my jaw and replied that my friend could always count upon my resolve. Holmes smiled thinly and confirmed he knew that to be the truth.

Presently our hansom drew into the salubrious area of Park Lane and within moments stopped outside one of the very grandest residences. The four-storey building was fronted by substantial columns on either side of the main entrance, and fine drapes hung at the windows.

We alighted. Holmes strode to the front door and pounded three times with the heavy wrought-iron knocker thereon. Only a few seconds passed before the door was opened and Holmes introduced himself to the doorman with a brusque, 'I am here to see the Duke, as requested by the card I sent last night.'

We were shown into a particularly grand entrance hall with polished marble floors, fine paintings and gilt mirrors tastefully placed at intervals along the walls. I glanced up to see a huge chandelier suspended above our heads and lit, it would seem, by the latest developments in gas.

Without ceremony, my friend and I were ushered into a lavish drawing room where a tall man with obviously aristocratic bearing was standing by the side of an ornately carved desk topped with unblemished red leather.

The doorman presented Holmes to the Duke with the words, 'Mr Sherlock Holmes to see you, sir, as he requested. Mr Holmes, may I present the Duke of Argyll.' After he retired from the room, Holmes immediately introduced me as his colleague. No hand was extended to either Holmes or myself, so I did not proffer mine.

'I am aware of who you are, sir and the nature of your business. I will say that I have little regard for those who busy themselves with the affairs of others. However, I have noted that you have managed to claim a few victories for law and order over the years, so I was therefore disposed to see you despite the lateness of your request.' The Duke delivered his address with the almost unnaturally high, clipped tones of his class. His unwavering gaze remained locked upon the both of us, and I began to find the atmosphere of the room somewhat intimidating.

I am not a man to quail in the presence of others, but I must confess that the Duke had a certain manner that was most unsettling. It was as if centuries of breeding had produced a man whose demeanour allowed for little tolerance of any persons he deemed to be of a lower station in life's lottery. I admit that I took an instant exception to him, and I noted that we all remained standing rather than be invited to take a seat. Either the Duke expected the interview to be brief, or he preferred to use his full height as a means to further reinforce his dominance of the proceedings.

Holmes was not to be flustered or intimidated. 'I must assure you, sir, that I am here on a matter of great urgency and delicacy. My only intention is to ensure the continued wellbeing and fortune of Your Grace.'

'Well, man, get on with it. I am due to play a rubber at my club in half an hour so I have only a few minutes before I depart,' was the curt reply.

'Very well. You may have read of the deaths of a number of businessmen in France over the past several weeks. They died most horribly. What you may not know is they were also members of a secretive international society of financiers.'

If Holmes' revelation meant anything to the Duke, he gave no indication of it. 'Continue,' he instructed.

'It is my belief that those involved with this society are being systematically murdered for a reason as yet unclear.'

The Duke remained silent, his eyes still fixed on us both.

Holmes made his gambit. 'Further, I have reason to believe that Your Grace may be a participant in the aforementioned society and that your life may, at this very moment, be in the gravest danger.'

The Duke paused before answering as if weighing his response. 'Mark my words very carefully, Mr Sherlock Holmes. I am not, nor have ever been, a member of a society of the nature you describe. Your accusation is unfounded and may well be slanderous. I will have nothing further to say to you, sir. This interview is therefore at an end. Good day to you both.'

Less than a minute later Holmes and I found ourselves outside on the pavement, the heavy front doors already closed behind us.

'Let us take some air, Watson,' said my friend.

We walked in silence down the tree-lined avenue, the autumn sun glittering through the branches whose leaves had now mostly taken on those beautiful golds and browns of early October. We passed elegantly attired men and women, and luxurious coaches bearing their occupants in sumptuous comfort to and from the city. I recall being impressed by how even the cobblestones were of an even and uniform size and the pavements clean and almost polished.

When we were more than a hundred yards from the residence we had so rapidly departed, Holmes stopped and leaned against a tree. 'I expected as much. He is both a very brave and very foolish man. I fear there is little I can do for him now. He has made his decision and I am sure that no further entreaty I might make would meet with any greater success.'

'But surely, Holmes, the man must not want to lose his life over this, especially given that you may be able to help him out of this appalling situation,' I ventured.

'Although the Duke will not accept help, he has assisted us no end. Don't you see, Watson, he has confirmed that whatever dealings he has had with this society are so serious as to be impossible for him to admit to. He has chosen to risk death rather than face accusations, even privately from me. The significance of this cannot be overstated.'

I thought for a moment. 'So if we can identify a crime the society has been instrumental in...'

'We might be able to deduce who the murderer is!' Holmes finished my sentence. 'Well done, Watson!' He clapped me on the back. Although I could have been easily irritated by the somewhat superior tone he was apt to adopt at times such as this, I was pleased for a little levity after the unpleasantness of the morning audience with the Duke.

'I believe that least our next appointment may prove a little more civil,' said the detective as he hailed a cab and bade the driver make haste to Threadneedle Street.

I watched from the windows as we passed through Tottenham Court Road and then into the heart of the city itself where the great banks and insurance houses were located. At the very epicentre of an empire that spanned the globe, they were surely as powerful a symbol of Britain's might as have ever stood. The streets were thronged with messengers running this way and that, bearing slips of paper from one bank to another that pledged vast sums beyond the wildest dreams of even the richest men. These would be taken in credit as trustworthy as gold bullion. 'How many thousands must be changing hands here daily?' I mused to myself.

Evidently my companion had heard me. He leaned over and whispered conspiratorially, 'Not merely thousands, Watson, but maybe even a hundred million sterling.'

I could scarce comprehend such a figure, as I am sure no man could other than those who inhabited this formidable place and thought in sums large enough to change the fortunes of entire nations.

Our cab deposited us outside perhaps the most significant edifice of them all. The London Stock Exchange is a building that inspires respect from even the most rude and uncouth. It has a feeling of solidity that is greater than its age; it is a place that embodies the permanence and power of the British Empire like few others. It was with such thoughts of pride and humility at the accomplishments of our countrymen that I followed Holmes up the steps and into the expansive lobby.

The concierge quickly showed us to a capacious office on the second floor with a large plate-glass window that looked out over the main trading floor. I was amazed at scenes of what can only be described as chaos that were the hordes of share dealers. Despite the heaving mass below, I was aware that I could hear very little of what must surely have been a most oppressive din.

Holmes saw my interest and rapped the glass with his knuckle. 'Three sheets of glass, Watson, with a small space between to isolate sound. Most ingenious.'

A side door opened and a dapper little man of at least sixty years strode briskly into the office. His suit was undoubtedly of the very finest cloth that Savile Row had to offer and was cut in the latest style of the season. The large yellow carnation at his lapel stood in contrast to the dark material of his jacket.

'Gentlemen, please be seated.' He bade us to a pair of comfortable leather tubs before his desk while he sank into a beautifully tooled leather desk chair. 'I am delighted to meet you, Mr Sherlock Holmes – and I assume that you must be Dr Watson,' he beamed. 'I have followed a number of your cases with interest but I should say that in all honesty I never expected our paths to cross.'

A butler entered and placed a tray of pastries and coffee before us. I found myself beginning to thrill a little that such an obviously successful man should know me by name and his cordiality was a welcome contrast to our meeting earlier that morn. Although I am by nature a taciturn man, I am aware of experiencing a certain pleasure in being in a place of particular significance with persons of national import. I have often thought that this is a result of my army days when one placed such high esteem upon one's officers.

Holmes, however, was always completely unperturbed by an individual's status. I have remarked before that he has an unusual touch with those of all classes, and an ability to inspire trust and confidence in both the highest and lowest of the land. He seemed completely at ease as he addressed the man I recognised as the governor of the Bank of England.

'Thank you for agreeing to meet us away from your more usual office, Sir Peter. In the light of matters I wish to discuss, it is perhaps fortuitous that we should rendezvous here.'

'Nonsense, man! I keep this office here and visit at least twice a week. I hope I may be of assistance in your quest, whatever it may be?' The last words were spoken as a question.

'It is of a very grave and most delicate matter, Sir Peter. You may not know of the series of gruesome deaths that have befallen several financiers in our neighbouring country of France these past few months.' Sir Peter's expression changed not at all. Holmes then proceeded to outline the details known so far, sparing little other than the names of those three eminent Englishmen to whom I referred earlier.

'So what are you asking of me, Mr Holmes?' asked our distinguished host when my friend had concluded his discourse. 'You have made a good case for there being a collection of individuals operating as a morally corrupt society, but I suspect you require more of me than my agreement that this is so.'

'Indeed, Sir Peter. I request that you make some enquiries as to any possible large financial misdealings in the past several years. In particular, I am interested when there has been a very considerable benefit, whether by insurance or share dividend, as a result of a fire or

160

conflagration. I need to know about unproven rumours, whispered half-truths and insinuation.'

'I see. You are aware that repeating such rumours as you mention may amount to slander? Particularly given the nature of men you have mentioned who may be involved, and those names you have omitted of which I do not wish to be made aware at this juncture?'

'We must each rely upon the utmost discretion of the other, Sir Peter. After all, our motivations in this matter are both honourable and in accord. I must try to avert further destruction of human life, where you must work to avert a scandal that would see the gravest damage in living memory to the reputation of the City and the country.'

Sir Peter steepled his fingers and remained immobile for a good half minute. I fancied I could hear some of the commotion from the trading hall in the intervening silence. Then our host stood. 'Agreed, Mr Holmes.' He spoke quietly but assuredly. 'I will be in touch after I have made my initial enquiries.'

Minutes later we were in a hansom tripping back to Baker Street. Holmes was deep in thought; I knew not to interrupt at such times so busied myself with observing the subjects of Her Majesty as they went about their daily business. As we passed Pall Mall, Holmes turned to me and muttered, 'I think we shall find the sorriest tale at the heart of this matter, Watson. A most sorry tale indeed.'

'Why did you specifically request Sir Peter to consider fires in his enquiries?' I asked. It seemed to me that my friend had made one of his leaps of intuition and I wished to understand his reasoning.

'Well, Watson, one of the features of this case is that the victims are most horribly burned. This is no coincidence and would add a considerable complication to matters for the murderer. Let us suppose that the burning of the bodies has a greater, or even symbolic, significance and the murderer is making a statement or perhaps sending a message by his method of execution. Not for him the gun or the sword or poison, or any of a hundred other methods of despatching a human being from this world to the next. No, Watson, the key to this investigation lies in the methods chosen by the perpetrator. Therefore, it is not difficult to hypothesise that there is symbolism in what he does.'

I found myself bound to agree with my friend's reasoning. Once Holmes had elaborated upon his thought processes, it was hard to see how any alternative could be countenanced.

'I think it likely that fire is a central theme to the entire case,' he continued. 'It is not difficult to surmise that a society involved in matters of great finance that has fallen foul of an assassin might have set these events in motion through a fire, either deliberate or negligent in the first instance.'

'And therefore,' I added, the gruesome conclusion to this discourse ever more apparent, 'your theory will be confirmed through the death by burning of the Duke of Argyll.'

'Precisely so, Watson.'

We spent the remainder of the journey home in silent contemplation of the impending and horrible death of a man that we could do nothing to avert.

*****

The next few days saw few developments of any note and I divided my time between our Baker Street rooms and my practice. Sherlock Holmes spent considerable time abroad in our bustling city. I suspected that he was speaking with his innumerable contacts and monitoring the movements of the Duke as closely as he could. He had obviously employed those keen-eyed little ragamuffins as he had done in many cases previously, for several times an urchin was ushered before me by a disapproving Mrs Hudson to deliver a message to 'Mr 'Olmes' when he returned. Invariably the messages were of 'nothing to report'.

It was on the fifth day, shortly before breakfast, that a commotion on the stairs signalled a development. Three lads were escorted before us. 'Bobbies everywhere, Mr 'Olmes,' said the largest of the boys. His companions nodded vigorously in affirmation.

''Bout twenty minutes ago, the butler comes out of 'is Lordship's 'ouse and shouts for the police. Whistles were blowin', and next thing more coppers was running up the street. Just before we left, an inspector arrived.'

Holmes congratulated the boys on their diligence and solemnly handed over what looked like a whole guinea.

When our guests had departed, I turned to Holmes and suggested that I might get my coat for I was sure we would be hurrying over to the Duke's house without delay. 'On the contrary, Watson. I think we shall wait here and enjoy our breakfast.'

I confess I was a little surprised at my friend's response, but the smell of bacon that came seeping under our door soon convinced me not to protest. It was no more than half an hour later, just as we were finishing a fortifying strong coffee, that we heard the front door open. Within moments, footfalls hurried up the stairs.

Holmes raised an eyebrow and stepped to the door, opening it smartly just as Inspector Lestrade reached it. 'Do come in, Inspector. May we offer you some refreshment? I see you have wasted little time in getting here from the Duke of Argyll's residence.'

Lestrade, florid from his exertions, started. 'Aha! Mr Holmes, you have already confirmed that you have an involvement in this! You have unwittingly asserted that you have knowledge of events that occurred not an hour ago, yet you obviously have not yet left your rooms!' He nodded at the remains of our repast, as yet uncleared from the table.

'Quite correct, Inspector. I have just moments ago received word of a great commotion at His Grace's house,' said Holmes suavely. 'I thought it would not be many minutes before my friend Lestrade was on my doorstep asking me why I had visited the Duke not several days previously.'

'You admit it then!' cried the little man.

'Indeed I do, Inspector. I visited the Duke in connection with this tragic matter but, alas, was unable to convince His Grace of the gravity of the situation. Further, he commanded me to take no further action on the matter.'

'Mr Holmes, a most eminent man has been slain this very morning. I must insist that you tell me all you know without delay and without recourse to those riddles to which you so often resort.'

If Holmes was annoyed at the man's impertinence, he did not show it. 'Of course Inspector. Please be seated and I shall tell you all that I know to be true of this case.'

For the next quarter of an hour, the eminent detective delivered a discourse that was devoid of any speculation or theory but, while entirely factual, did little to cast light upon the events. When he had finished, Lestrade announced his intention to review Yard files of known murderers and assassins and left, his brow furrowed in deep thought, but agreeing to the suggestion that Holmes should continue to look into the matter.

'Holmes, surely you misled the inspector!' I found myself greatly concerned at the details my friend had omitted, which included the names of the other two figures of national import.

'Hmm, Watson. This case is so delicate that I am convinced that Lestrade blundering headlong into it would have the most undesirable consequences. I have therefore done exactly as I promised and furnished him with the information I know to be true, which is rather little at present. I have, I'll warrant you, kept most of my theories and speculation to myself at this juncture.'

I confess I was not reassured by this and Holmes could certainly see my troubled countenance.

'Fear not, Watson. I shall ensure that Lestrade has information enough to help prevent another tragedy. As soon as the moment is appropriate, I shall include him in my findings completely and without reservation.' For the next hour, Holmes sat in silent contemplation then he scribbled some telegrams and sent Mrs Hudson to ensure their dispatch.

Less than an hour later we faced the Duke's house again, but this time in the knowledge that the illustrious owner would never again receive guests. The front door was guarded by two burly policemen, while a knot of pressmen begged them to reveal details of the tragedy.

The arrival of Holmes and myself did not go unnoticed. Within moments the great detective was surrounded and we were being jostled in a most unseemly fashion. 'Mr Holmes, what is your interest in this gruesome murder?' and 'Dr Watson, what brings you and Mr Holmes here?' My friend brushed them aside and, after a brief word with the policemen, we were permitted entrance to the hallway where we were met by Lestrade and a deputy.

''Tis most perplexing, Mr Holmes,' Lestrade said. 'He's in the garden. Apparently, it was His Grace's habit to walk a while before breakfast.'

Without breaking stride, Holmes followed the inspector into the drawing-room in which we had endured our interview, through a pair of open glass doors and into the well-kept gardens. Less than a dozen paces away we discerned a human form under a blanket. A police sergeant stood in attendance conversing quietly with a man I recognised as a police surgeon.

My colleague motioned the sentry aside and reached down to pull back the blanket. The face and torso of the Duke, still in a smoking jacket, were revealed. His eyes were open and there was an unmistakable look of shock and horror upon the dead man's face.

Holmes froze and then slowly straightened up. His tall, angular frame appeared all the more striking in contrast to the pitiful, prone form before him. 'This isn't right,' I heard him mutter. 'Not right at all.' He wheeled and addressed the police surgeon. 'How did he die?'

The surgeon, whom I knew by reputation, was immediate in his response. 'Single, fatal stab wound to the heart.' He leaned down and gently opened the Duke's jacket to expose his chest. 'There!' He pointed to a deep red stain that had spread across the man's chest.

Although a single injury, it was clear the blade had been driven home with uncommon force. I suddenly found myself feeling rather chill, despite the mildness of the morning.

Holmes surveyed the garden then, without a word, made a quick circuit, stopping several times and muttering to himself. In little more than five minutes he returned and pointed to a wall overgrown with ivy. 'The murderer climbed over that wall at about six o'clock this morning. He hid himself behind that tree,' he gestured to a solid-looking birch with a stout trunk. 'When he saw the Duke, he approached him directly without running and administered the fatal wound. He watched his victim die

167

and stifled any attempts by the Duke to cry out for assistance. Death was mercifully quick.'

'I had thought as much myself, Mr 'Olmes,' said Lestrade immediately. ''Cept I don't know how you can be so sure he approached 'is Grace directly. Surely he could have surprised him.'

'On the contrary, my good Inspector. From where we find the body, we can see the murderer's footprints clearly in the soft earth of the border. The steps were regular and at normal walking speed, as can be seen by their distance apart. There was nowhere for him to hide, and besides he didn't want to. The victim knew him and recognised him, and our man wanted the Duke to see who had slain him.' He paused. 'I take it, Lestrade, you have already questioned the staff and nobody saw or heard anything?'

The inspector nodded.

'There are many clues here but I need time to reflect upon their meaning. Gentlemen, I bid you a good day.' When he saw Lestrade look perturbed, Holmes continued, 'Be assured, Inspector, I shall share my thoughts with you as soon as I have put them in order.'

Our ride home was a silent one and I left Holmes sitting in his chair while I went to attend to some patients. It was later that evening before I returned to find my friend had not moved.

After a few minutes, Holmes looked at me and spoke. 'This is most odd, Watson. Some of the facts are so obvious as to be almost deliberately so, while there are inconsistencies that indicate a most complex chain of events to lead us to this point.'

'You mean why wasn't the body burned, for a start?' I ventured. I had thought of little else than the events of the morning since we had departed the Duke's house.

'Yes, that is one concern. The assassin – for it was a carefully planned and bold killing – had plenty of opportunity to apply a flammable liquid to the body and ignite it. For some reason he did not. By the same measure, it is likely that the previous victims died as a result of immolation because no autopsy has shown any evidence of stab or other wounds, although I'll grant you they could have been missed. Further, I believe that the significance of fire is central to this case, that the murderer wishes his victims to be burned to death, and that he gains satisfaction from that gruesome act.

'In this instance, the perpetrator has changed his modus operandi. We must discover why in this instance he did so, or wait to see whether the method of dispatch for the next victim shows a return to the previous form. In the meantime, I must busy myself with experimentation and trial. I know you have matters to attend to, so shall we say dinner here at eight?'

As it was, my practice had been a little quiet for some weeks so I spent a thoughtful afternoon taking the air in the environs of Hyde Park before returning home and attending to some correspondence.

At a little before eight I returned to Baker Street. As soon as I entered the hall, I immediately became aware of the most awful stench. It was a smell I was not unfamiliar with, having witnessed death by burning during my time in Afghanistan.

Mrs Hudson appeared looking both distressed and disapproving, as only she could. 'He's taken all the pork and brisket I had in the larder and sent me out for more. Mr Watson, he goes too far this time. I dare say the neighbours are suffering this almost as much as I am!'

I grimaced and bounded up the stairs two at a time, our housekeeper's strident tones still ringing in my ear. I opened the door to be confronted by the most hideous atmosphere. The air was laden with smoke and the smell was quite appalling. I felt the bile rise in my throat as I strode to the window and threw it open.

I turned to find Holmes regarding me gravely. 'Good grief, Holmes, how can you stand to remain here?'

He didn't answer but turned to the table upon which were numerous scraps of burned and charred meat. 'It is extraordinarily difficult to set flesh on fire, Watson. The liquid content virtually prevents it. Yet the victims so far have been burned throughout and even their internal organs have shown fire and heat damage. There.' He passed across a bundle of papers, which I discovered were copies of autopsy notes. I thumbed through the sheaf and it was as my friend suggested: in most cases where the examination had been thorough, there was evidence of internal heat damage.

'I have never seen the like,' I admitted. 'It is very difficult to imagine how such damage could be inflicted. One would expect the immolation to proceed from the outside inward, not from both exterior and interior at the same time.'

Holmes agreed entirely. I insisted that we dine at Mortimer's that eve, given that the atmosphere of our rooms was still most unpleasant and Mrs Hudson was now sadly lacking a main course due to my friend's researches.

Mortimer's was busy as was usual for such a fine establishment. The clientele comprised discerning diners and businessmen intent upon wooing new contracts. The décor, while elaborate, was most tasteful and I was always impressed by the new electric light the management had installed only the previous year. To my eye the light was softer and more even than gas and, of course, had the amazing benefit of being switched on and off instantly. Indeed, throughout the evening the waiters were obliged to give demonstrations to various interested patrons who clapped their hands with delight and declared it a wonder of the modern age.

Holmes was not the best dinner companion that evening as he appeared considerably distracted. He ate slowly, sometimes appearing to forget to swallow so that his tenderloin must have been so thoroughly chewed as to be tasteless. Every few minutes his gaze would travel back and forth between the electric bulb above our table and the nearest waiter who was providing yet another demonstration of the unique properties of electric light.

Our meal, while devoid of much in the way of conversation, was pleasant enough; I can thoroughly recommend the curried pheasant if you are ever passing by. Our journey home did not follow the most direct route, for Holmes asked the driver to take us via the Embankment. He offered no explanation. When we reached the river, my companion leapt from the cab and strode directly to one of the nearby lamp posts, recently installed and powered again by that mysterious force that had illuminated our repast earlier that evening.

For several minutes the famous detective stood immobile, bathed in the crisp white light of the street lamp. His gaze turned upward and his sharp features were thrown into stark relief by the incandescent glow.

I was struck by how his motionless frame reminded me of a man who was experiencing an epiphany. I suppressed a chuckle but, when Holmes returned to the hansom, I could not resist. 'So, Holmes, have you seen the light?'

My companion stared at me for a few moments and then replied quietly, 'You know, Watson, I think I might have.'

Upon our return to Baker Street, a telegram was waiting for us. Holmes confirmed it was from Sir Peter. My friend rummaged through his files and clippings until I heard a triumphant 'Aha!'

I was just reaching for another cigar when Holmes glanced up and said, 'Pack your bags, Watson, and make arrangements for tomorrow we leave for America.'

Part Two

We arrived at the Liverpool docks shortly before midday, having spent four hours dashing through the English countryside in a first-class carriage on the 7.14 express from Euston.

During our journey, Holmes revealed that the previous evening's telegram had provided details of some irregular financial practice concerning a very large insurance payment resulting from the 1890 fire that had destroyed a swathe of New York. Sir Peter had provided the name of an eminent financier who had been implicated but against whom no case had been brought. However, the detective also furnished me with a fascinating, if rather macabre, article concerning a new method of execution our American cousins were now employing – that of electrocution, or death by electricity.

After reading the piece, I was forced to agree that such a method might cause some of the effects that had been visited upon the cadavers of this case. Holmes intended to meet proponents of the process and to discover if electricity could indeed be the method employed by our murderer.

After we had passed through the ticketing office, we stepped onto the quayside of the Albert Dock. I must confess that my jaw dropped and rendered me a most comical sight. Holmes grinned at me and we both stood a moment to take in the magnificent spectacle that was before us.

The new White Star liner, the RMS *Teutonic,* towered over us. The sleek lines of her colossal superstructure loomed more than a hundred feet above our heads. Everywhere there was activity as porters and passengers swarmed around the gangplanks that led into the depths of the great ship.

Her two great funnels were already belching steam as her huge boilers were brought up to pressure, and I marvelled at the immense power that must be needed not only to move such a vast vessel but to propel her at more than twenty knots across the great expanse of the Atlantic Ocean. Indeed, this monument to man's ingenuity did much to banish the unease I had been harbouring regarding another example of an invention that involved a novel means of execution.

The feeling of wonder only grew upon entering the ship. Everywhere was furniture of the highest quality, the fixtures of gleaming brass and gold plate, the carpets thick and luxuriant, and the fittings of finest maple, walnut and other exquisitely tooled woods.

We were shown to our adjacent cabins by a smartly dressed porter resplendent in the livery of the line. Our cabins were joined by an internal door and within moments Holmes appeared. 'What ho, Watson! how do you find your quarters?'

I looked around the spacious cabin complete with its sitting area, large bed and porthole and professed it was entirely dissimilar in every respect to the troopships I had endured during my army days.

*****

We passed the voyage uneventfully but most comfortably. The food was excellent, the wine and liquors exemplary, and I fancy both Holmes and I rather over-indulged in the fine cigars on offer. As is my wont, I slept soundly and copiously. Holmes, intent upon the case, roamed the ship or retreated to his cabin for hours on end.

On the second night we played some blackjack and I have to say I found the game quite thrilling. Holmes, of course, treated it as an intellectual exercise and soon amassed a tidy sum, at which point he grew bored and retired to the ship's library.

The mighty engines never ceased their thrumming and soon a rumour began to circulate amongst the passengers that the captain was trying for the Blue Riband. It certainly seemed as if the colossal ten thousand tons of the *Teutonic* were hurling themselves with unmitigated fury against the implacable Atlantic.

On the sixth day I awoke to a cacophony of sirens, whistles, hoots and bells. Scrambling to my feet, I threw back the curtain from my porthole. Through the thick glass, I could see buildings on the shore creeping past. I quickly pulled on some clothes and, without waiting to tie my cravat as I would normally do, I dashed from my cabin, nearly colliding with a steward, and out onto the deck.

Already there were many passengers leaning on the rails waving, laughing and some enthusiastically toasting our arrival. Holmes was standing motionless at the rail, staring intently at the crowd gathering on the quayside. The small flotilla of boats in attendance sounded their horns as the *Teutonic* manoeuvred majestically toward the dock, huge ropes snaking from her sides to the insect-like tugboats that laboured to turn her massive bulk. The two fireboats aft made a fantastic spectacle by turning on their powerful pumps and issuing arcs of spray, the droplets creating rainbows much to the delight of my fellow travellers.

The city of New York loomed behind the bustling docks and the Hudson seemed to sparkle in the early morning sun. I fancied that the air smelled sweet, a heady mixture of salt and smoke, and I found myself breaking into a smile.

I was struck by how different this arrival in the New World was from those not so many years past. My companion and I had traversed the most difficult and treacherous ocean on the planet in complete comfort in less than six days. How our forefathers completing those gruelling feats of maritime endurance would have marvelled at our progress.

I turned to Holmes intending to remark upon such matters and observed that faraway look that in the past has so often indicated great mental effort on his part. Thus I decided to enjoy the moment and await his acknowledgement.

It was then that a great cheer went up from the quayside. I was to learn that our fine vessel had indeed taken the Blue Riband with a time of just five days, sixteen hours and thirty-one minutes, a most splendid conclusion to a successful crossing.

*****

As we descended the gangplank to the quay, I observed a gentleman hurrying toward us, his hand outstretched. 'Holmes! Watson! How splendid to meet you both!' Quickly we were introduced to Sir Peter's representative, a man named Jefferson whose beaming smile made us feel immediately welcome.

Holmes and I both extended our hands, which were warmly shaken. Our host ushered us to a waiting taxicab hauled by a fine chestnut gelding. Within moments we had left the teeming docks behind and were hurrying towards the epicentre of the great metropolis that some say will rival our own great capital before the next few decades are out. I was most impressed by the scale of construction underway and the gleaming new electric trams that passed us almost noiselessly at a not-inconsiderable speed.

Our guide pointed out features of interest, including a most interesting building called The Tower. He informed us that this had used an entirely new construction technique in that a steel frame was built first then the brickwork added over the top. This ingenious method allowed for much greater height in building as the load was spread throughout the structure rather than directly upon the floor below. Jefferson told us enthusiastically that there were plans being drawn up for yet taller buildings using this same process.

Without a doubt, New York struck me as perhaps the most energetic city I had ever visited. Whereas London conveys a sense of immense history and solidity, its American counterpart was being built literally before our very eyes. Our cab drove us down elegant Park Row and I marvelled at the brand new twenty-story New York World Building; at over three hundred feet in height it was truly a wonder, and a very visible statement of ambition from the New World.

Holmes, often withdrawn in thought during carriage rides, also gazed out with interest. 'Our American cousins are most certainly an industrious people, Watson.' I nodded my agreement and my companion continued. 'To have achieved so much in so little time makes one wonder what they will do with the world in the coming century.'

Our driver pulled up at the Hotel Normandie on the corner of Broadway and 38th Street. We bade our guide farewell, with Holmes promising to call on him if his services were needed. Clearly Sir Peter's generosity was nowhere near exhausted, I thought, as we entered the splendid foyer and notified the clerk of our arrival. I noted with some chagrin that the owners boasted that the building was fireproof.

I was not entirely surprised to find that a telegram was already waiting for my friend. The contents plainly had significance as Holmes remained thoughtful and aloof over dinner until we retired at ten.

*****

The next morning a cab and driver were already waiting for us after we had breakfasted. Knowing that Holmes would reveal our destination when he chose, I sat quite happily looking out of the window and taking in some more of the splendid sights. Soon we alighted at the magnificent Central Station, there to take a train to the town of Ossining, Westchester County, about thirty miles distant.

Holmes sat in silence as the countryside rushed past and in less than an hour we were once again aboard a cab that was waiting to collect us.

'Electricity is a funny thing, Watson,' my friend mused.

I started. 'Indeed it is,' I agreed.

'What is it, Watson?'

'I beg your pardon?' I replied.

'What is electricity?'

I looked at Holmes slightly bemused and aware that I had limited knowledge in this respect. I conveyed my confusion to my companion.

'Exactly, Watson. No-one really knows what it is. A force of some kind is the best explanation scientists have been able to come up with. Yet it is seemingly everywhere and, unless I am much mistaken, it is soon to become an indispensable requirement for modern living. Our homes will be lit by it, labour-saving appliances powered by it, our trains driven by it, our streets illuminated by it and perhaps even our bodies cured by it. And yet no single person has been able to provide an adequate explanation of what it is. We are putting our trust, and soon perhaps our very lives, in the hands of a mysterious force of which we understand very little. Doesn't that strike you as a little odd, Watson?'

I listened to Holmes' soliloquy with fascination. I had to agree that electricity was a cause for concern, although I ventured that surely its powers for good weighed far in excess of its dangers.

'I am not so sure, Watson. We shall see,' was the detective's thoughtful response.

Our cab had apparently arrived at our destination. I was more than a little taken aback to realise it was perhaps one of the most notorious places on Earth. It was a prison whose name was known even across the great expanse of the Atlantic: Sing Sing.

A small crowd of people, some well-dressed and some in more humble attire, milled about the principal entrance to the forbidding edifice. Some carried placards that appeared to denounce execution, and a few stood holding candles conducting a silent vigil.

Our cab drew up outside a smaller door, though it was still massive in its construction, and after a few words a guard admitted my friend and me. Clearly arrangements had been made and we were expected. After a few minutes wait in a small anteroom, we were joined by a sombrely besuited man who introduced himself as the governor of the establishment.

'Gentlemen, you have made good time and are about to witness the application of a new technique. It is the most humane method of meeting the ultimate sanction, and I trust you will be satisfied with the result.'

'Holmes!' I whispered urgently as we were led down a maze of whitewashed corridors and passed rapidly through one heavy door after another. 'You did not mention we were to witness an execution!'

'Indeed I did not, Watson, for I was not sure that we would arrive in time. But steel yourself, for this may be a most significant and informative event.'

Not for the first time I found his apparent coldness disagreeable. To Holmes, this was little more than an experiment to be observed and catalogued. Although I had seen much suffering during my time in Afghanistan, and even witnessed summary executions of deserters, I am a doctor and it is my sworn duty to preserve and cherish all human life as the most precious thing of all.

Our host was speaking to Holmes as we strode down yet another corridor. 'Harris Smiler is a convicted murderer. The state has decreed that he will be the first of four men who will depart this mortal coil today. Ah! Here we are.'

We emerged into a large room devoid of all furnishing, save for a strangely crafted chair set against the wall at one end. A door on the opposite wall stood closed.

Perhaps twenty people, whom the Governor assured us were comprised of the local judiciary, persons of influence, and the family of the victim, stood silently but with clear expectation.

I noticed that upon entering the room our host gave an almost imperceptible nod to a colleague. Within moments the door was flung open and a man was brought through, held and flanked by two guards. A priest followed closely behind.

Immediately the man was manoeuvred to the chair and heavy cuffs of steel were placed over his wrists and around his ankles. Leather straps were bound tightly across his arms, groin and chest as the cleric intoned the last rites. A black hood was placed over his head and a metal cap, apparently with water running through it, was put over his scalp.

The guards stood back and turned to another official who was standing at a panel, the centrepiece of which was a large lever. At a word from the governor, the switch was thrown and the figure in the chair went rigid, his arms and legs straining against his shackles in a dreadful spasm of anguish. The switch was reversed and the man slumped. Again it was thrown, and again the body convulsed in a most grotesque fashion. Again the current was reversed. A man clearly identifiable as a doctor stepped forward and quickly checked for a pulse before retiring some distance, and for a third time electricity coursed through the pathetic figure in the chair.

This was obviously sufficient for, when he checked again, the physician pronounced the man dead in a clear voice and noted the time. The chair had completed its horrible work.

A subdued murmuring broke out the witnesses and the sickly-sweet smell of scorched flesh could be discerned. The hood was removed and Harris Smiler's lifeless face was revealed. I will save the reader from some of my more gruesome observations at this juncture, but suffice to say the catastrophic effects of the electrical current were immediately apparent. A number of people stepped forward to examine him, perhaps kith and kin of his victim, but after a few minutes a sheet was draped over the corpse and we were ushered out.

Holmes remained. He crossed the room to engage the executioner in a discussion. I signalled my intent to leave and, without a backward glance, I made my way from that dreadful place.

*****

I didn't rejoin Holmes again until later that afternoon when he found me sitting in a nearby hostelry. His mood was sombre and matched my own. For long minutes we sat contemplating the inferior brandy that had been set before us.

'It has been a most educational day, Watson. I have witnessed three further executions, each without undue event. But, while I believe I may have made some progress in this investigation, there are still many aspects of it that elude me.' It was unusual for Holmes to be so candid as to his vexation. For a moment I saw a man who had experienced a day that, while of intellectual interest, had not left him unmoved.

I nodded slowly. 'I think I would like to return to our hotel, Holmes.'

'Agreed, Watson. So would I.'

*****

I saw little of Holmes for the next two days. My companion spent his time in the public records' office, the coroners' courts and various other offices of local business. After the unsettling visit to Sing Sing, I resolved to walk about the city. I visited Central Park, which I found delightfully tranquil; I went to the New York Museum of Natural History, which, while not yet comparable to the glorious British museum of the same name, did show promise; I took a boat ride out to the Statue of Liberty, a true marvel dedicated not five years before but already a symbol of the United States across the globe.

On the third day Holmes received a telegram at breakfast. Upon reading the contents his face became grave and he said, 'I think our time here is drawing to a close, Watson. There has been another murder – a prominent politician, no less. His charred remains were found by Blackfriars Bridge.'

We were to remain in New York for two further uneventful days until the next available passage. I was pleased to find that it was once again the *Teutonic*, ready for her return voyage across the mighty expanse of ocean that separated two countries that appeared similar to me in many ways but were so very different in a great deal more.

I bade New York farewell, hoping to return someday at greater leisure, and turned my head eastward towards the Atlantic and home.

Part Three

London in August was sultry, basking in baking heat by day and a stifling stillness at night. Ladies carried parasols and gentlemen struggled to maintain even the most basic standards of dress. The Serpentine was a Mecca for those seeking the succour of cool water and swimming, and I determined to spend an afternoon there as soon as I could.

Holmes, however, appeared impervious to the temperatures. His energy seemed to increase as the mercury climbed past ninety, while my thoughts were preoccupied with visions of lemonade and water ices.

It was a little over a week after we had returned when news reached us of another charred corpse, this time found by a carriageway in Hyde Park. The deceased was the owner of a wealthy stockbroking firm whose name I did not recognise. Holmes and I were attending to other matters that morning concerning the disappearance of Lady Carmichael's favourite parrot, but at my companion's instruction, we drove past the Bank of England, where we admired the grand carriages and beautifully turned-out horses from which gentleman of substance alighted before climbing the steps of Sir John Soane's masterpiece.

As we passed the grand entrance Holmes turned to me. 'Watson, I have made progress. I believe I may have identified the murderer and I have some ideas as to his means, although I admit some practical elements still elude me. Nonetheless, I have informed Sir Peter that I am confident of a successful resolution to this case.'

'I say, Holmes! That's splendid news!'

'I fear not, Watson, for I am convinced that I will be unable to apprehend the murderer before his work is finished. He is not only a most unusual assassin; he also enjoys considerable protection from formidable powers.'

'But that has never prevented you prevailing before,' I challenged my friend, most perturbed to hear his qualification.

'Perhaps not, my dear Watson, but this time I also have some sympathy for his cause.' Holmes paused, his hooded eyes more serious than I had seen them for a long time. I waited.

'I shall explain what I believe to be true, Watson, and you shall be good enough, as you always are, to question and probe.' I nodded gently.

'It is a tragic affair, Watson, most tragic. It involves the death of a bright young family and the revenge of a loving father.'

I loosened my cravat and leaned forward in my seat.

'From the first it was obvious that we were dealing with a shadowy organisation whose activities have been often nefarious and frequently illegal in most civilised countries. The members of this sordid syndicate were extremely rich and powerful members of society, and some were well-known public figures. It was also obvious that the assassin must also be a man of considerable resource, high intelligence and deadly nerve – exactly the kind of man who might become a member of this secret society had he not a more evolved morality.'

'I say, Holmes, that does indeed make perfect sense.'

The detective nodded slowly. 'Further, he had a most profound motive. What could that be? Money? Unlikely; a wealthy man may gain and lose much money in his lifetime but he is rarely without assets of some description, and in times of dire need his equally wealthy friends will ensure he is looked after.

'Love, then? Although I sometimes grapple with understanding this emotion, I do concede that it is the most powerful one of all. A man who has lost his wife may be driven to drink or self-destruction, but if he has his family he will most always pull himself around for their sake. But what if he has lost all that he loves at the hands of those he trusted and worked with, and whose secrets he had kept? How terrible would be the betrayal, Watson, and how dreadful would be his revenge.'

Despite the heat of the late afternoon, I felt a chill come upon me. 'Such a man would not stop until his retribution was complete,' I observed.

Holmes looked sharply toward me. 'I have no doubt you are correct, my friend. No doubt at all. And yet I have sympathy for him for he is bereft of the family he loved so dearly and he knows precisely who killed them.

'Watson, the roots of this case lie a year and a half ago in a dreadful fire that destroyed several blocks of brownstones in Manhattan. This fire was deliberately set, and it was done for nothing more than financial gain. This abhorrent brotherhood of financiers had agreed a plan to profit by millions of dollars from the destruction of the heart of a city. More than a hundred souls perished, including the young family of a certain Corbin Rake, the heir to the Rake Bank fortune. Corbin only escaped by sheer chance. Up to that point he had worked at Rake Bank developing his professional practice. He had only recently been introduced to the syndicate by his father, Albert Rake, a most ruthless financier who himself has since perished a little over a year ago in a house fire that was thought at the time to be accidental. Needless to say, it was not.

'Albert was a senior figure in this network and had probably spent decades helping to build and nurture it. Albert was, in fact, *Albert* with the French pronunciation of the silent T, and was born a Frenchman of wealthy stock. Thus this vile cabal has, as our good friend Philippe suspected, its roots in that country. In point of fact, I believe much of the original money that formed the foundations upon which Rake Bank was built came one way or another through the activities of this group of men.

'I am also quite sure, although I admit that this is mostly speculation on my part, that the younger Corbin was an honest and brilliant man who rejected this initiation and threatened to bring the whole shoddy organisation down. For this reason, almost certainly with his father's acquiescence, he was to die. The fact that his family would also perish was little more than a detail. In the ultimate betrayal, his father chose to destroy him and his wife and children rather than risk exposing his collaborators.'

'How utterly monstrous! Holmes, the world would be better rid of these men. I can scarcely believe what I am hearing!'

'I would find it difficult to disagree with you, Watson,' said Holmes grimly.

We returned to Baker Street in thoughtful silence. Holmes was no doubt turning the case over and over in his mind, analysing it from every angle and weighing theories against probabilities. I, on the other hand, felt a deep sadness at the depravities of which some men are capable in the pursuit of riches and power.

My countenance must have betrayed me, for Holmes scribbled a telegram as soon as we reached our rooms and called for Mrs Hudson to dispatch it. Then he spoke. 'I think it is time for us to draw this matter to a conclusion, Watson. A carriage will arrive for us shortly. I would be pleased if you would ensure you are carrying your revolver. I shall furnish myself with this sturdy hatchet.' My resolute expression must have satisfied him because he sank into his chair and calmly filled a pipe, gesturing for me to do the same.

It was a little over an hour later when our housekeeper called out to inform us that our transportation had arrived. The carriage was sumptuous and of exceptionally sturdy construction. I noted that the interior was softly lit by an incandescent bulb and I could make out Holmes, who sat opposite me, staring at it with a look of intense concentration. 'Be ready for action, Watson,' he said, 'for I expect our carriage to stop presently.'

I was about to reply that I was prepared for anything when the carriage halted abruptly and I heard the driver climb down from his perch. At that moment I heard a distinct click and, to my astonishment, it started to rain inside the compartment. In an instant Holmes launched himself from the seat and lunged for the door handle, wrestling with it in vain as he tried to turn it. 'Shoot the lock, Watson! Shoot it now!'

I pulled my revolver from my coat as the bulb began to fade and took aim in the hellish confines of our prison. I fired twice and then again, my shots splintering the heavy wood of the door. Holmes tried again but the door refused to give. The hatchet appeared in his hand and he hacked and smashed violently at it.

I became aware of a strange burning sensation starting up my legs and rapidly increasing in intensity. 'My God, Holmes...!'

He didn't turn but with one last mighty blow shattered the glass and the window frame surrounding it, kicked the door open and pulled me out onto the cobbles.

We both lay for some moments on the unyielding stones, trying to gather our wits and our breath. Then Holmes was up. 'Come on, Watson, we have him in our sights!'

A figure was sprinting away, covering the ground at a ferocious pace.

I tried to run but my legs would not submit to my command and I staggered and fell. I saw that Holmes, perhaps ten yards ahead of me, was also in difficulty and had to stop. Pulling myself up, I reached him and placed a hand on his drenched shoulder of his jacket.

'Curses! We nearly had him! But it matters not. We can now bring this appalling matter to its rightful end. Come, Watson, we have one final appointment that we must fulfil.'

*****

Holmes drove the carriage in silence, making full use of his encyclopaedic knowledge of the highways and byways of our great city that equalled that of any London cabbie. Presently we drew up outside a large and imposing residence in a most salubrious part of Mayfair.

Holmes rapped loudly upon the intricately carved front door. Within moments there was the sound of a heavy bolt being slid back and a butler's face appeared in the gathering evening gloom. 'Tell Sir Peter I will see him immediately,' commanded my companion.

'Is he expecting you, sir?'

'Almost certainly not,' said Holmes, and pushed past the protesting servant. 'Aha! Sir Peter! We will talk with you now.' The small figure of the governor of the Bank of England had appeared at the end of the imposing entrance hall and gestured toward the door of his salon.

If he was surprised, Sir Peter hid it well. 'Please do sit down, gentlemen. I know why you are here and I have no wish to add to the discomfort you have both suffered.' Our host sank into a green-leather winged chair. He looked at Holmes evenly, and I reminded myself this was a man who was accustomed to wielding power and confronting matters most men would quail at. 'You have important matters to relate to me. Tell me, when did you work it all out, Mr Holmes?'

'While in New York I concocted a working theory based upon some very specific research, but it was only this evening that I gained confirmation that my surmises, astounding as they may be, were almost entirely accurate.'

I admit I was still trying to make some sense of what had transpired, but I knew that Holmes was masterful in these situations. And so he was as he laid out the entire dreadful story to the man who had been implicit in our near demise not an hour earlier.

'When the venerable Inspecteur Grimaud first made me aware of the deaths of some wealthy and connected members of a secretive society of financiers, I realised that not only was the method of execution – because execution it most certainly was – entirely unprecedented but that I was up against a powerful and unprincipled foe who would stop at nothing to protect their sordid secrets.

'Based upon a partial list of possible victims, I made haste to warn the Duke of Argyll that he was in desperate peril. His refusal to acknowledge the danger confirmed to me the gravity of the crimes of which this brotherhood was guilty, although the manner of his death nearly threw me. He died of a single stab wound to the heart, not by immolation as with the previous victims. When I examined the body where it had fallen, I noted that the wound bore clear indications that the blade had been first plunged with considerable force into the Duke's breast.

Then, as he died, it was twisted violently as the killer undoubtedly looked into his victim's eyes.

'This was the first instructive clue in this complex and ingenious case. It was obvious to me that his executioner had wanted to see His Grace suffer; this was a man hell bent on revenge who would take satisfaction from the final agonies of his enemy. I wondered what it was that led to the Duke being slain in such a way, and then I realised that it was us, Watson and myself. *We* were the difference. None of the other victims had been warned, and the Duke, despite his dismissal of us, had in fact listened and taken precautions by remaining in his house and garden rather than venturing out.

'However, it was the strange state of the other corpses that proved the most difficult to resolve. The post-mortem results indicated a pattern of burning that I have never seen before, nor has it been detected in other cases whereby souls have perished by fire. I began to wonder how such terrible wounds could be inflicted. My researches led me across the Atlantic, where our inventive cousins have started trials of a new scientific method of despatch, the terrible electric chair.

Holmes turned to me. 'After the electrocution of the hapless Harris Smiler, I attended an immediate dissection of his body. I observed indications of the same effects as noted in the post-mortems of the victims brought to our attention by Inspecteur Grimaud. Thus I felt my theory had been proven; the method of execution was by electricity. In the case of the Westinghouse Edison design, this is delivered in short, very energetic bursts, thus despatching the criminal quickly. Whereas in the case of our victims, death almost certainly came more slowly and more painfully as it was the intent of the perpetrator that his victims suffer.

'Which brings me to Corbin Rake.' Sir Peter started in his chair and Holmes held up a cautionary hand. 'There is no point in protesting. I know who the killer is, and I understand his motivation.

'Corbin was a brilliant young man with a family and a full life ahead of him. His wife and three children were robbed of that future by the schemes of men devoid of compassion who cared not for such matters, but pursued wealth at any cost. I also know, Sir Peter, that you were aware of, or had your suspicions about, the identity of some of these venal creatures. Albert Rake had made overtures to you to join them. I am certain that you not only rejected his offer but found it to be repulsive.'

Sir Peter's eyes dropped, and he nodded gently. 'I did, Mr Holmes. I do not profess to be a man devoid of vices and vanities, and I have made mistakes and enemies in my life, but I have not and never would have participated in the kinds of schemes that Rake and his dreadful organisation were ready to undertake.'

'This I know. It is the reason why I am talking to you now in your home rather than in an interview room at Scotland Yard,' said Holmes carefully and deliberately. 'You knew something of the scheme to burn several blocks in Manhattan, but you could not prove or prevent it. When the dreadful plan was put into action and the fire spread out of control claiming hundreds of innocent lives, you were appalled. But it was when you learned of the deaths of a young family in particular that you decided to act in collusion with a man who had lost everything.' Holmes paused. 'Your godson, Corbin Rake.'

Sir Peter's eyes moistened and his voice cracked. 'Yes, you are right. The lovely Celia, his wife, and their children, Maggie, Daisy and Benjamin...' His voice trailed off. 'They were all very dear to me and I thought of them as my own family to a much greater extent than that undeserving brute Albert ever did.'

'When Corbin, bereft with his loss and determined to bring justice to those who had caused the deaths of his family without so much as a moment's troubled conscience, came to you for help you were ready to stand with him.' Said Holmes sombrely. 'You devised the most ingenious plan to ensure they suffered slowly, as had his poor wife and children. They were to die agonising deaths through being burned alive from within, in a manner that only this recently harnessed elemental force could provide.

'But although I knew the means by which they were killed, I still couldn't divine the method by which the executions were delivered – until I saw your carriage outside the Bank of England. There was something amiss about it that only a trained eye might discern, but at that moment several pieces of the puzzle fell into place. I noticed that your carriage had certain unique features. It had exceptionally large leaf springs, of a type usually only found on vehicles carrying a great weight, and there appeared to be a large case fixed to the roof that I now

196

realise was there to hold many gallons of water. The weight of your carriage was, therefore, a result of the concealment of certain unique features, namely a huge reservoir of water and many high capacity batteries.

'These devices – the water to aid conductivity, the batteries to deliver a continual electrical charge, an iron grid in the floor and triple-paned windows such as I observed in your office at the Stock Exchange – were confirmed to me as Watson and I rode in the carriage sent by you in response to my telegram earlier this evening.

'I was certain that our driver was none other than Corbin himself. To save him from exposure before he could complete his revenge and destroy an organisation you believed the world would be better off without, you and he decided that Watson and I must be prevented from completing our investigation, even if that meant our deaths.'

Sir Peter looked at both Holmes and me. 'I am sorry, gentlemen. Please believe me that it brought me nothing but anguish to arrive at that dreadful impasse.'

Holmes nodded and I also believed him. 'But how,' I interjected, 'would the Duke have been made to travel in your carriage had Holmes and I not intervened?'

'I can answer that,' said Sir Peter. 'I was not aware of His Grace's involvement in all this until quite recently but he and I often played bridge together at our club. I would have simply invited him to join me and sent my carriage to fetch him. We have done the same many times in the past.'

'Of course, you and he were friends,' Holmes confirmed. 'And so the betrayal was even greater. This web of iniquity is so truly encompassing, turning man against man, and for what? A few more bars of bullion?'

'So what do you propose, Mr Holmes? If you so wish it I will confess, but I will not give you Corbin. He has suffered enough and is now on his way to a safe place far away where I will ensure he is provided for and he shall have a chance at building a new life.'

Holmes sat for a full minute in thought and then he rose. 'Come, Watson, our business here is concluded. Sir Peter, I am certain you will already have arranged for the disposal and destruction of your carriage, and I can prove none of this fantastic tale beyond reasonable doubt. I must therefore trust you to be a man of integrity who will use all the legal powers at your command to ensure this appalling cabal never re-forms or recovers. In turn, I give you my undertaking that I will not trouble Corbin further.'

And with that, we departed. The kerbside was already empty and the carriage nowhere in sight.

'Let us walk a few moments, Watson.' Holmes sighed heavily. 'There are no victors in this case, and no heroes, but more than a-plenty of villains. I see little to be gained from further action on our part; indeed, a man such as Sir Peter is perhaps our best ally against these shadowy forces. This has been one of our more challenging cases, and yet I do not feel a sense of satisfaction at its conclusion. Perhaps I will in time, but not tonight.'

I agreed most emphatically, ignored the dull ache in my leg and hailed a cab in the sincere hope that there might still be time for some supper.

Author's Note

The stories of Sherlock Holmes and Doctor Watson have given me, like countless millions of others across the world, great enjoyment for many years.

I first discovered Conan Doyle's greatest literary creation when I was just twelve years old. After persevering with the occasionally challenging prose I found, much to my joy, the cleverest and most perfectly plotted stories I had ever read. I thrilled at the *Silver Blaze*, struggled to sleep at *The Hound of the Baskervilles*, and cheered at his resolution to the *Musgrave Ritual*. I still recall vividly my despair at Holmes apparent demise at the Reichenbach Falls while battling Moriarty in the *Final Problem*, and my unbridled joy at his resurrection before an overcome Watson in *The Adventure of the Empty House*.

I have written widely for many purposes over the years, both commercial and pleasure, but during all that time there was a little voice urging me to pay homage to the greatest detective the world has ever known.

My own son is now twelve years old. This volume is my most humble attempt to emulate the style and substance of Conan Doyle and to give dear Sherlock a few more cases to solve.

Printed in Great Britain
by Amazon